Heart in a Bottle

by: Lisa A. Tippette

DEDICATION

To Ginger, my beloved fur-child

who will always have a special piece of my heart.

R.I.P. Sweet Girl!

Heart in a Bottle

by: Lisa A. Tippette

Chapter 1

Valli Heart stepped out behind her handcrafted, oak-barrel desk and walked over to the trio of large picture windows facing out. The view was breathtaking. Pastel blue skies with sunlit streaks of teal cascaded high above the vast sea of blue and green below. In the distance, colorful sails outlined in white drifted silently by with the grace of angels, carrying her soulful thoughts along with them. A brilliant, beaming sun illuminated every square inch of the glistening coastline, where sea birds played tag with the waves and sea treasures washed ashore to be discovered by passing shell hunters. Out of all God's wondrous creations, nothing was more hauntingly beautiful than the sea, and she felt incredibly blessed to have a job that afforded her such an amazing view. And proud. She had worked SO hard to achieve the pinnacle of success that included such a priceless view, although for her, it had come at an enormously high and personal cost.

Her thoughts drifted away to five years earlier when her precious Daddy succumbed to a massive heart attack. Being an only child, and the proverbial "apple of her father's eye", his sudden death threw her into an emotional tailspin. She had lost her mother to cancer just a few years before that, and never having married or had children, was left all alone in the world, save for some distant relatives scattered around here and there, whom she rarely saw.

She was also sole heir to the family business, Heart Winery, and left to carry on her father's lifelong dream of growing it into a successful and flourishing wine empire; a daunting task for a middle-aged advertising exec who knew very little about the sophisticated complexities of running a major corporation. And even ι loved him with all her heart, it seemed her father had left her ε. shoes to fill, along with an even bigger hole in her heart. At times, burden seemed almost impossible to bear.

Valli was mad at the world, madder still at her father for leaving ι and even angrier with God for taking him. But despite all that hurt and anger, and her often wavering faith in God, she still had a relentless determination to succeed. If for no other reason than for her sweet Daddy. She was all he had left. His sole heir. She knew it was up to her to carry on his legacy and try to make Heart Winery everything he had dreamed of.

So, she pushed through those mentally, spiritually and emotionally dark times with grit determination, and without a clue as to where she was going, much less in which direction to go. She blindly walked in faith, and stumbled many times along the unfamiliar, rocky path. And when she found herself lost, afraid and alone, she cried out to God with a David-like faith and humbled herself to Him. Without fail, He always led her back to solid ground. And now here she was five years later, a successful businesswoman carrying on her father's work and literally enjoying the sweet "fruits" of her labor, thanks to a God who faithfully walked by her side and never let her down.

She turned her attention back to the magnificent view in front of her and whispered a grateful prayer of thanks to its Creator. One weighty, lone tear escaped from her eye and she quickly wiped it away. As usual, the evil demons from her past were quick to appear, haunting her idyllic moment, and robbing her of even one minute of happiness. She was not surprised by their uninvited presence. It happened every time she got close to the precipice of happiness. In fact, it seemed like there was always some kind of powerful struggle within her keeping her from being truly happy, and she longed for a time when her mind - and heart, could be at peace at the same time. As fulfilling and prosperous as her life was, why wasn't well-earned success, and an amazing ocean view not enough?

Why did the haughty demons of her past still dwell unwelcome in her mind, and cause continuous turmoil in her heart and soul?

There could only be one reason; a secret shame that had haunted her for nearly twenty-five years. A shame she wished she could drown in the darkest depths of the ocean or send on a one-way trip back to the fiery depths of hell. But it kept coming back – like a crashing wave slamming the defenseless shore, receding only long enough to gain strength, and then bear down on her battered soul again and again.

She laughed a weak chuckle to herself at the irony of it all. That she should choose a home by the ocean where stormy seas often served as a constant reminder of the restlessness within her. Yet, when she gazed out at low tide, and saw the calm and peaceful waters rolling effortlessly in and out, she knew that likewise, one day, God would bind those torturous demons, and finally calm the raging storm in her soul. And THEN she would have genuine peace – the peace that only He promises in His Word; the peace that can overcome even HER relentless demons.

"Daydreaming again, Ms. Heart?" The rude, interrupting voice behind her belonged to Jack Conova, her junior business partner, and the man to whom her father owed much of Heart Winery's current success.

Although she had a well-earned four-year marketing degree, Valli knew very little of the complex wine making business her father had so abruptly passed onto her. Fortunately, a few years before his death he had the wise forethought to hire Jack, a fresh out of college business major, well-seasoned world traveler, and most importantly, well-trained connoisseur of fine wines. He had spent his senior year in college studying at the European Wine Academy in France, where he discovered his passion for the wine industry, and unique skill in crafting designer wines. After graduating college, he returned home to Crescent Beach and used his crisp, new diploma and worldly charm to persuade her father into hiring him as an intern at Heart Winery, promising him he would turn the paltry vineyard into a "wine mega-tropolis". He spoke with resolute assurance the auspicious words her father longed to hear, and Jack was hired almost immediately on the spot. Valli, however, was more guarded, and always suspected it was Jack's truer intention to cunningly worm his way to the top of Heart Winery, and ultimately control her father's business. In short, she was certain he had his eyes on HER job!

Over my dead body, she repeatedly proclaimed, remembering the secret vow she made to her father after his death – that NO ONE would EVER gain control of Heart Winery, except another Heart family member. And since there weren't a whole lot of them standing in line for the position, Valli made it her mission to honor, protect and guard not just HER job, but the entire company from the likes of Jack Conova! It was the only thing she had left of her father, and she wasn't about to give it up to some "wet behind the ears" college kid, even if he WAS an expert sommelier!

Jack, however, made a lasting impression on her father, delving head-first into the day-to-day operations of the small winery, and working tirelessly to brand it into a household name – locally, at least. In fact, he single-handedly developed two award-winning reds that landed the small coastal community of Crescent Beach, home of Heart Winery, on the proverbial wine map, as well as on the cover of Coastal Wine magazine, a top leading local industry publication!

Looking back, Valli had to admit that it seemed God had directed Jack's course in life to collide with theirs, for the uncertain times to come. And even the egotistical, big headed college boy himself admitted he felt led in his spirit to seek out Heart Winery, though there were bigger wineries he could have chosen. A perfect example of God's words: *"A man's heart devises his way: but the LORD directs his steps."* (Proverbs 16:9 KJV)

After her father's untimely death, Valli knew she couldn't run the business competently without Jack's wine knowledge and expertise, so she promoted him to junior partner, in charge of the vineyard production and operations, while she managed the more creative marketing and advertising end of the business from her panoramic ocean view office. The vineyards and operating facility were just a few miles down the road, but since she lived on the far end of the beach, she rented an office nearby for convenience – and the picture-perfect view, of course!

"Who can resist daydreaming with a view like that," she soulfully replied, still lost and consumed in the ocean's hypnotic trance. If only the ocean could hide her shameful secrets in its depths, the same way it hid unknown mysteries!

Jack moved closer to the window where she stood and peeked over her shoulder. "It's a great view alright, and perfect weather for growing award-winning grapes to make award-winning wines! Whoever said you couldn't grow grapes by the sea didn't know a grape from a coffee bean!"

Valli turned to face him. "Hey, Mr. Genius – I've got a newsflash for you: wineries all over this coast are growing grapes by the sea – there's nothing so unusual about THAT!" She hoped her sarcasm would shoot down his over-active egotism – one of Jack's lesser attractive qualities.

"Ah, but not just ANY grape!" he smugly corrected her. "I was the one that convinced your father that the Syrah grapes would do well here, while all the other wineries were only growing Chardonnays and Zinfandels! I knew from my wine studies abroad that the Syrah grape was made just for climates such as this, and I couldn't wait to get back to Crescent Beach to try it out for myself! And now, after years of trial and error, I've not only PROVEN it, I've developed the NEXT award-winning Syrah wine varietal – one I'm SURE will come in FIRST PLACE at the Crescent Beach Wine festival this fall! I just KNOW my Blue Merlot is going to win out over ALL the others!"

Blue Merlot was Jack's newest varietal, blended from the savory Syrah grapes he had encouraged her father to grow due to their affinity for producing well in coastal regions. It was a secret proprietary blend of Syrah and other grapes, that held subtle hints of black cherry, dark chocolate, and other secret ingredients that Jack refused to divulge. In fact, he had the recipe secretly hidden until the wine festival was over, where he was SURE he would take top prize! No doubt it was an aromatic bouquet, and he assured her it would be unlike anything the judges had ever tasted!

Valli suspected his melodramatic excitement about winning first place in the upcoming wine festival was also because of the extravagant grand prize - an all-expense paid trip for two to the Barossa Valley Winery of Southern Australia, home of some of the oldest known vineyards and wineries in the region. Ever since Jack developed Blue Merlot, it's all he talked about. How he longed to visit Barossa and introduce it to the local wineries there, and co-create an imported version using their own vintage Syrah grapes.

Such a spectacular grape would give my Blue Merlot blend a velvety body, richer tannins, and that sought-out wine grandeur all great wine enthusiasts look for, he claimed. Not to mention it would put him in circles of influence he'd only dreamed of, giving him the financial clout and status of the elite and famous.

If there was ever a man that relished fame, fortune and pretty women, it was Jack Conova – notoriously dubbed "Jack-so-nova" by all the bitter ladies whose broken hearts had littered his doorway – and his bedroom. Despite all his shrewd business sense and well-trained wine palate, Jack may have been a talented wine maker, but he was a lousy lover, never seeming to be able to find the "right blend" in his relationships with women, as he did with his wine.

Yes, to travel to Australia was his "big dream" - a dream more intoxicating than the wine itself, and Valli knew Jack was determined to make it come true - at ANY cost. Unfortunately, Heart Winery wasn't financially stable enough to afford Jack such a lavish trip, nor could they spare him at the vineyard - especially since her father had died. His dream of skyrocketing success, and hob-knobbing with the rich and famous in Australia would just have to wait until the company was in better financial shape - unless he happened to win the grand prize at the wine festival.

Valli jolted herself back to reality and sat back down to tackle the mound of paperwork piling up on her desk. Jack stayed by the window, lost in his own carefree daydreams of fame and fortune.

"Blue Merlot is a good wine, Jack, but it takes more than that to win. I've got to get busy on this marketing campaign if we're ever going to be ready to present it to the local market first. That's MY priority right now – Australia will just have to wait in line with all the other countries you want to conquer."

"Oh, don't be such a kill-joy, Val! I've got an award-winning wine this year and you know it! I'd put my Blue Merlot up against any other snarky wine of its kind without a moment's hesitation. My heart and soul are in that bottle of wine, and THAT alone makes it priceless!"

Jack always referred to her as "Val" when he was in one of his extra-cocky moods, which she could do without now. She glanced up just long enough to catch a cheesy wink after his remark, but ignored his egoism, and reiterated her previous point with a touch of her own snarky sarcasm.

"Try to keep your feet on the ground, Jack - and your head out of the clouds. There's going to be some stiff competition at the festival this year, and we're still considered amateurs compared to some of the more established wineries that will be there. I'm sure your "heart in a bottle" creation will be sought after in every corner of the world one day, but for now let's just focus on building our brand and making Blue Merlot a LOCAL sensation, okay? Now, was there anything else you wanted?" Picking up on her subtle hint to leave, Jack walked up behind her, bent down and whispered a flirty remark in her ear.

"Not now, sweetheart. You just have your bags packed and be ready to take that red-eye the day after the festival because you and I are going "down under" baby, and we're BOTH going to come up ON TOP!" He pressed his lips heavy against her naked alabaster skin, and very gently ran his warm tongue lightly down the nape of her neck, causing tiny goose bumps to quickly break forth, and ripple wildly throughout her body. She wanted to reach back and slap him to the moon, but before she could sync her brain with her hand, he had strutted arrogantly out the door. She reached behind her and grabbed her neck. It was still disgustingly wet and warm from his touch.

Going down under; come up on top.

Jack's words always did seem to have a slight sexual undertone to them. Clearly, he was coming onto her. Again. Nothing so unusual about that, though. Like many other women in Crescent Beach, she, too, had once had her own "one-night fling" with Jack Conova, and it ended badly. VERY badly. Yet another fateful night. Another demon she carelessly let take up residence in her soul. For the sake of the company, they had both agreed NOT to ever talk about it, but it didn't stop Jack from reminding her what she "could have had" every chance he got. Nevertheless, she still had her doubts about his intentions, and had NO desire to rekindle any romantic sparks with a man she was certain wanted to steal her company.

Not that he wasn't attractive enough; that young and innocent boyish charm perpetually frozen in a hot and sexy grown man's lustful words. Those dark, dreamy brown Italian eyes that could make her blush every shade of red in a paint store with just a friendly wink; those prominent Cherokee-Indian high, stone-chiseled cheek bones, and a muscular fit and sleek toned physique – what woman WOULDN'T be enamored with such an irresistible hunk? If only his personality ranked as high as his looks.

Valli let out a hopeless sigh. What a shame to be SO good-looking, and yet SO self-centered! God surely blessed him with good looks and intelligence, but Jack must have slept late the day He was giving out humility!

Still, as much as she hated to admit it, Jack had been a Godsend to her – especially when her Daddy died - stepping up to the plate and working hard to take Heart Winery places her Daddy had only dreamed of going. She smiled thinking how proud her Daddy would be of the success she and Jack had attained since his passing, and she knew in her heart that Jack was a BIG part of the reason WHY Heart Winery was on such a successful path. It was also a big reason WHY she tolerated his "cocky come-ons".

Nevertheless, she couldn't shake the nagging feeling that Jack's "Casanova charm" was all part of his conniving strategy to win her over, and eventually gain controlling interest in Heart Winery. After all, she had total control of the business, and without her blessing, he couldn't travel very far in his quest to rub elbows with the rich and famous! He knew he had to play her just right to get what he wanted, and he was just scheming enough to pull off the perfect plan.

Business-wise, she reluctantly trusted Jack to do what was best for Heart Winery, even if he, himself had selfish motives. But she couldn't afford to gamble away her father's company by letting Jack take full control of the reins. EVER. So long as she was living, Heart Winery would remain in her TOTAL control, even if she didn't know what she was doing. Thankfully, she DID have a trusted Board of Advisers that were handpicked by her father, and she knew they would guide her along on the things she didn't have the knowledge or experience to know how to handle.

Heart Winery was all she had left of her sweet father, and there would NEVER be another man that could fill his shoes – period. That was even more reason she needed to keep her head clear and her mind focused on business – NOT romance. She owed it to her father to take care of the only legacy he had left her. Besides, with shameful skeletons rattling in her own closet, Valli had to keep a tight rein not only on her heart, but her mind as well, lest her own restless demons escape and make her life a living hell.

No, unlike Jack's secret blend in Blue Merlot that was meant to be opened, poured in a wine glass and savored, it was best to keep HER fragile heart and scandalous secrets locked safely away in a tightly sealed bottle- maybe even for the rest of her life!

Chapter 2

Valli awakened the next day to the thunderous boom of an early morning storm. Stretching her neck like a giraffe, from her bedroom window she could see the angry waves crashing against the jagged rocks that dotted all the way down to the far end of the north shore. The skies were murky gray and overcast, and the wind squalls were gusting just enough to rattle the metal awnings that covered the windows of her 1950's style beach house.

Her father had bought the old concrete cement block house for her after she graduated college, and had it updated with a new roof and reinforced windows and doors to withstand the sometimes harsh and unrelenting nor'easter storms that were a common occurrence with coastal living. The old place had managed to hold up remarkably well, and she likened it to the strength God had given her to withstand similar ruthless storms she had faced in her own life.

But no matter how hard the storms came pounding down on her, God always seemed to pull her up in His lifeboat – safe and sound from the unforeseen dangers that lie in the murky waters of her troubled life. As she listened to the wind's empty howl, and the copious rainwater splash angrily against the bedroom windows, she knew that this storm, too, would soon pass.

Another deafening clap of thunder shouted at her from the heavens, as if God was saying *GET UP, VALLI*, knowing what a slumberous sleepy head she was on mornings like this. Ignoring God's heavenly alarm clock, she shut her eyes tight, and wiggled further down in the covers to try and capture a few last-minute winks. But it didn't take long before a troubling dream quickly came to life in her semi-altered state. More like a nightmare, as the demons of her past promptly took center stage. The scene was the same as it was twenty-five years ago. Same people. Same place. Same tragic ending…

"NO! NO! DON'T DO IT, VALLI, PLEASE!" the shrieking voice echoed mercilessly in her head like a thousand crystal chandeliers shattering on a glass floor.

The haunting voices and vivid images of that horrible night jolted her awake, and she sat straight up in her bed. Heavy beads of sweat had formed on her forehead and neck, and her hands were as cold and clammy as a teenage boy on his first date. Trembling and breathless, she reached over and grabbed the bottle of pills that rested on her nightstand. Her "sanity pills" as she called them. Without them, she was a helpless victim, without warning, to the terrifying memories that often plagued her otherwise sane existence. Dr. Jacobs, her therapist, had prescribed them to her a few years ago, when the flashbacks and nightmares started, and she had kept her prescription filled religiously since then. She didn't necessarily like having to depend on sedatives to help her get through the day, and she prayed every day that God would heal her from her "thorn in her flesh". But like the Apostle Paul, her prayers for deliverance went unanswered day after day; year after year. True, God had given her His grace to withstand her "infirmities", but sometimes she wished for more than just grace. Like peace of mind. Or deliverance. Yes – all she wanted was to be delivered from the constant torture of a reckless past.

She quickly gulped down two of the tiny pills and washed them away with the watered down leftover tea, she had left sitting on the nightstand the night before. She didn't know which tasted worse – the bitter pills or the weak tea. She swallowed hard and prayed the pills would kick in soon. A second glance at the clock urged her to drag herself up from the warmth and security of her king-sized bed. It would have been so easy to cocoon herself in the freshly washed linen-scented sheets and let the pills work their magic, but Jack had asked her to come to the winery first thing that morning to give a marketing presentation to a local yacht club owner who was interested in carrying Blue Merlot as a private label wine in his high-profile yacht club. She had stayed up late the night before perfecting the presentation and was excited at the possibility of acquiring such a prestigious client.

Seth Spencer, owner of the Crescent Beach Yachtsman Club, was a friend of Jacks, as well as a prominent businessman in the community. His yacht club was first-class, and it would give Heart Winery another notch in the "oak barrel bedpost" if he chose Blue Merlot as the private label wine for his club. Of course, for Jack and Valli, it would mean "hobnobbing" with the upscale and affluent yacht club members on occasion, but she could hold her nose up as high as they could if it meant success and prestige for Heart Winery!

She often thought of how ironic it was that he should inherit a wine business, considering the damage alcohol had done to her family. She had her mother to thank for that. The woman was a pathetic alcoholic and social embarrassment to her and her father, not to mention the reason Valli was left with such an insurmountable burden to shoulder the rest of her life. And although she knew she should forgive her mother, she found it very hard to have compassion on the woman who once put her young, teenage daughter in such a shameful AND dangerous situation. All because she was stone cold drunk! If only her mother had stayed home and not gone out drinking that night...

Once more, haunting memories of that fateful night shot through Valli like fur standing up on the back of a Halloween cat. She quickly tore out of bed and jumped in the shower in hopes of drowning out any lingering effects of her early morning psychosis. She opted for a quick, cold shower to chill the fiery memories, and ward off the drowsy effects of her sanity pills. After getting dressed and downing a half pot of heady Italian espresso coffee, she finally felt ready to face the dreary, oppressive weather on the other side of her front door.

As was her usual custom on her way to work, she lifted a quick prayer to God to bless her day with sound business sense, guide her through a successful presentation with this new client, and give her wise judgment to make the right decisions for Heart Winery. She also asked once more for peace of mind, and for God to destroy the unrelenting demons in her soul before they destroyed her. It was a prayer she prayed daily, but she was confident that one day He WOULD answer it. In His timing.

The hot, late-summer August sun was quickly burning off the early morning fog, and likewise, the cold shower and strong coffee Valli had earlier was finally clearing her head and driving away the gloomy thoughts that had awakened her. Her mind was clear and bright as her sullen mood lifted from dismal to delightful. The sanity pills were finally kicking in, and even though she knew it was a "false sense of happiness", at this point, she'd take whatever form of it she could get. Besides, she'd masked her true feelings for over twenty-five years and these days she hardly even knew WHO she was anymore.

She turned down the long, grape vineyard lined road that led to Heart Winery. The orchard vines were hanging full of dark, plump, luscious Syrah grapes and she could almost taste the sweet, juicy nectar hiding in each fruity cluster. She remembered as a little girl, her father would put her on his shoulders and let her pick the grapes at the top of the grape vines. *Those were the most perfect ones because they saw the sunrise FIRST*, he used to say. Her Daddy knew the sun was the secret to the sweet, yet tangy tartness of the grapes, and only the most perfect tasting grapes went into a bottle of Heart wine. She remembered eating as many as she picked, but her Daddy never scolded her for it. He'd much rather seen her stuffing a handful of grapes in her mouth rather than a cookie or chocolate bar.

Even now, she preferred a fresh fruit salad over a decadent dessert when dining out at a restaurant. It was also the reason she could keep her five-foot-five petite figure from expanding into the shape of a busted can of biscuits! Of course, all the stress in her life (both personal and professional) boosted her metabolism into a high efficiency calorie furnace and helped her stay trim, not to mention all those back-to-back high stress days when she just plain "forgot to eat"!

After taking a park in front of the building, Valli took a last-minute inspection of her appearance. Her attire was casual yet colorful - just a comfortable pair of Bohemian-inspired paisley printed palazzo pants with a flirty, teal blue ruffled-tiered sleeveless blouse. Over-sized, black-peace sign earrings dangled from her ears and peeked through her champagne blonde hair, while rainbow colored bangle bracelets jangled cheerily around her wrists. A pair of three inch strappy, cross-toe gladiator wedge sandals in a matching teal color completed her funky ensemble.

Valli was secretly a "hippie" at heart; a child of the peace-loving sixties era, with the wanderlust soul of a free-spirited gypsy girl. Only her soul hadn't been allowed to wander free much since that formidable night twenty-five years earlier. And although she wasn't necessarily a "tree-hugger", she had always loved nature, and the ocean. Nothing made her feel closer to God than taking a long, meditative stroll down the beach, or a soul-searching walk through the red, yellow and golden carpet of fallen leaves in the quiet solitude of the wooded forest in fall. She considered her love of nature a precious gift from God, and a trait that was further instilled in her by her father.

The son of a cotton farmer, her father Daniel Heart, had worked the land since he was old enough to climb on a tractor with his own daddy. Together, they spent endless summer days tilling and planting the same acres that Heart Winery stood on today. In fact, his daddy had the very first coastal winery on Heart Hill (as it was known back then) in the 1800's. Some called it just plain ole "bootlegging" back then, but Granddaddy Heart knew the same secret her Daddy knew — how the sun shone just right on Heart Hill to produce the sweetest, most flavorful grapes in all Crescent Beach. And while everyone else was teasing Granddaddy Heart and telling him how foolish he was to try and grow grapes in the sand, he knew he was on to something. He trusted his instincts - and more importantly God - and worked tirelessly to prove them all wrong, although he would never live to see in real life what he could always see in his dreams.

When Granddaddy Heart died, her father took over the family business with the same tenacious ambition, instinctive know-how, and headstrong determination his daddy had instilled in him, and kept the family business going. The very fact that Heart Winery was still standing while all the others fell by the wayside, was a rock-solid testament to the conscientious work ethic of the early Heart family pioneers who paved the way. And now, with no other heirs to pass the torch on to, it was Valli's responsibility to keep the family business fires burning long and bright.

But having no siblings meant Valli was "daddy's little girl", and the father-daughter bond they shared was nothing short of untouchable. Even her mother had jealous fits of rage whenever Valli would spent long summer days roaming around the vineyards with him or hanging out in the wine cellar when he was making his special homemade "grape juice", as it was so discreetly referred to back then. He'd always save some of the fresh squeezed grape juice and make Valli her own blend of "kiddie wine", kept in Mason jars in the refrigerator. Whenever her parents indulged in a glass of "adult wine", her father would always allow her to join them with the special "kiddie version" he made for her, poured in a fancy wine glass, of course! It was only after she got to be teenager that she learned the stark and sometimes painful difference between the "adult wine" and her "kiddie wine".

She remembered with much sober detail, when she was about sixteen, how she and her best friend Casey got into a bottle of the "real stuff" in the cellar, and got crazy, cross-eyed drunk. Her father had gone to a business meeting, and her mother was asleep on the couch, when she and Casey decided to venture down to the wine cellar and sample some of the newest varietals of wine her father had just bottled. Figuring it couldn't be any stronger than store bought grape juice, they poured themselves generous glasses, refilling them often before they were even empty. As the alcohol ran freely through their bloodstream, they began to dance and stumble around the room, laughing and giggling after every sip. They were so drunk, they never even heard Valli's father drive up a few hours later.

Unannounced, he came busting in on them as they were refilling their glasses for the umpteenth time. Furious and disappointed in their sinful disobedience, he gave them both a good tongue-lashing for going in the wine cellar without permission, as well as a forty-five-minute lecture on the formidable consequences of overindulging on alcohol. He then promptly took Casey home, and grounded Valli for two weeks. The next day, Valli's head felt like it was two sizes too big for her body, and she spent a good part of the morning hugging the porcelain. She barely remembered the lecture her father had given the night before, but after hours of puking her guts out 'til her eyeballs turned inside out, she swore NEVER to drink another drop of wine again! And although he hated seeing his daughter suffer through the lingering pangs of a wretched hangover, he knew it was a valuable lesson she'd learn amidst all that gagging and puking. Too bad her mother didn't learn the same lesson. She always claimed she never had a "drinking problem", but she sure wasted herself on some awful hangovers!

Valli glanced at the clock on the dash. It was almost showtime! She took a quick moment to freshen her pale nude lipstick in the rear-view mirror one last time and squirted a hefty mist of minty breath spray in her mouth. She couldn't wait to dazzle her new client with her most brilliant AND surprising ad campaign yet!

Chapter 3

"Val, come on in, you're right on time! Jack was uncharacteristically cordial as he ushered Valli into the conference room. "I'd like you to meet Seth Spencer, owner and captain of the very prestigious Crescent Beach Yachtsman Club! Seth, meet our CEO, and daughter of the founder of Heart Winery, Valli Heart."

Valli smiled warmly and extended her hand to Seth's. He returned a pearly white toothy smile, clasped both his hands around hers and gently squeezed them. "It is a great pleasure and honor to meet you, Miss Heart, or is it MRS. Heart?" he asked with a flirting wink, still holding her hands prisoner in his firm grip.

"The pleasure is all mine, and it's MISS Heart." She cast him a taut smile, and quickly withdrew her hand from his unyielding handshake.

Jack Conova might have been a "looker," but Seth Spencer was Absalom reincarnated; *from the sole of his foot even to the crown of his head there was no blemish in him.* (2 Samuel 14:25 KJV)

His golden Tahitian sun-kissed face (an obvious perk from frequent yachting) encapsulated two sultry, ocean blue eyes and cheeky movie star dimples, accented by his wavy dirty blonde locks and neatly coiffed matching mustache. He stood a good six by six, yet stepped light and easy, carrying himself like a gentle giant. A pristine white, button down oxford shirt peeked out from a neatly pressed, navy monogrammed Yachtsman's Club jacket, and his well-fitting stone-washed Levi jeans perfectly outlined his sexy, toned buttocks. Valli was instantly star struck!

His eyes remained fixed on hers in a hypnotic gaze, and she was sure she was committing a cardinal sin just by looking at him! She wasn't used to being in the company of such wealthy, influential and drop dead, good-looking men, as she left most of the pretentious client meetings up to Jack. He reveled in that kind of environment, whereas she often felt like a cheap bottle of imitation grape juice in a Napa Valley wine cellar! But she knew how important this client was to Heart Winery, and to Jack, so she put on her best wine snob face and played along for the good of the company. Jack and Seth took a seat at the conference table, while Valli hooked her laptop up to the overhead projector and prepared to give her marketing presentation.

"So, Miss Heart," Seth started, "why should I make Heart Wine the exclusive wine of the Crescent Beach Yachtsman Club"?

His question was openly challenging, and despite Jack's last-minute notice, Valli had prepared one of her best presentations. She was pumped up, and ready for the challenge. She didn't care WHO he was, she intended to "dazzle and delight" him with her creative advertising and marketing skills and win over HIS heart to Heart Winery!

For nearly an hour, Valli extolled the fine virtues and exclusive features of Heart Wines, and the Blue Merlot collection, in particular. Her presentation was flawless. Nearing the end, she nervously shuffled around the room toward Seth, as she prepared to give him the final sales pitch – a late night thought that she hoped would bring in the winning run! Like a cunning lion stalking its unsuspecting prey, she moved in closer, made eye-to-eye contact, and cornered him with a sexy, confident stare. She could smell the sweet blood of success and was fearless in her words.

"In closing Mr. Spencer, it comes down to this: we have a saying here at Heart Winery that epitomizes just how unique and special our wines are, and why they would fit in perfectly at the Crescent Beach Yachtsman Club."

Judging by the laser beam of light exuding from both eyes, Seth was visibly intrigued. "And just what might THAT be, Miss Heart?"

Valli glanced nervously over at Jack. She knew he wasn't going to like what was coming next, but at this point, his feelings didn't matter as much as the prominent client sitting in front of her. She just hoped he'd be able to control himself and let her get through the rest of the presentation without any knee-jerk reactions. Besides, she WAS the CEO and had proprietary ownership of EVERYTHING at Heart Winery – even slogans.

"Mr. Spencer, may I present to you the exclusive labeling and advertising slogan for the private label wine collection we have in mind for the Crescent Beach Yachtsman Club." She clicked to the next screen and watched as Jack's mouth silently dropped to the floor. It simply read:

"HEART WINES – WE PUT OUR HEART AND SOUL INTO EVERY BOTTLE WE MAKE"

She turned her attention back to Seth, searching his face for any sign of approval, agreement or acceptance, none of which she saw.

Oh, how I wish I had a couple of "sanity pills" right about now!

She could almost feel the concrete floor begin to tremble below the carpet, like an erupting volcano, and just knew at any minute it would give way and swallow her up like Jonah's whale! Just as she was about to scramble for the nearest exit, Seth Spencer broke the deafening silence that was the proverbial elephant in the conference room.

"Excellent presentation, Ms. Heart! And I LOVE that slogan! It's very impressive and thought-catching and complements our image very well! I've sampled the unique wines in this collection, and I already know how exquisite they are. This ad campaign was the perfect pitch! I am happy and honored to accept Heart wines as the NEW private label wine for my yacht club! Well done, Miss Heart, and congratulations! You and Jack have outdone yourselves AND gained a new client!" He flashed her a sexy smile, much to Valli's relief.

She politely collapsed in a nearby chair, then casually looked over at Jack in hopes of seeing the same glad face of approval. He gave her a quick wink, but she could swear she saw fire dancing behind those smiling eyes. All she could do now was wait for the fall out, which she was sure would come the minute Seth Spencer was out of the room.

Impervious to all the one-sided flattery, Jack casually walked over to the wine bar and selected one of their finest reds. "That's great, Seth! How about a celebratory toast?" Only his suggestion was anything BUT celebratory.

"Thanks, Jack, but some other time. I've got another appointment and I'm already running late. But why don't you and Miss Heart come by the club around eight this evening, and we can celebrate then – my treat!"

Jack cocked a raised eyebrow over at Valli for her response. The staunch look on his face told her all she needed to know. She returned a half-crooked smile, and quickly nodded in agreement. Anything to lessen the blow. He glanced back at Seth. "Sounds great, Seth – I'll bring a complimentary bottle of Blue Merlot!"

"That's perfect, Jack. I look forward to seeing you BOTH again tonight, then." He started to leave, then stopped for just a second as he walked past Valli and stared deeply into her eyes. "I'll say it again, Miss Heart; that was an awesome presentation! I am very much looking forward to getting better acquainted with the charming CEO of Heart Winery tonight!" He winked a naughty wink. She winked back on impulse. Jack just looked at them with an empty stare.

After Seth left, Jack walked up to the laptop and stared blankly at the screen. Valli quickly snapped back to reality, knowing he was probably about to blow a gasket. She immediately tried to avert an ugly confrontation by offering a half-sincere apology.

"I know what you're thinking, Jack, and before you say anything, I'm really sorry I didn't discuss using that slogan with you first. It's just that it came to me at the last minute and I didn't think you'd mind. I hope you're not upset with me." She gave him a weak, unapologetic smile, then started packing up her laptop, hoping he wouldn't brood over it too long. Instead, Jack's lips curled up on both sides as he broke into a huge Grinch-like grin.

"UPSET WITH YOU? How could I be upset with you, Val? Do you realize this campaign just helped us win one of the biggest customers in our company's history? It was a brilliant idea, and you're a

GENIUS, my dear!" His unexpected reaction suspiciously confused her, and her ears perked up for more as he continued talking.

"Oh, I admit I was surprised when I first saw it, but after seeing Seth's enthusiastic reaction, I couldn't have been happier! Besides, this is a "win-win" for all of us – me, you, Heart Winery AND the Crescent Beach Yachtsman's Club! Thanks to you stealing my little slogan, we're ALL going to be RICH, RICH, RICH!"

Valli was visibly taken aback. "I don't understand, Jack. What do you mean, "stealing your slogan?" I wasn't aware you had a copyright on it! That's being a little presumptuous, don't you think? I mean, I admit I should have talked to you about it first, but I didn't think you would mind since it WAS for the good of the company! And what do you mean, we're ALL going to be rich now? One yacht club account is NOT going to make us exactly rich, Jack!"

Jack started prancing all around her, flapping his hands and arms all up in the air like a wild chicken in a half-crazed attempt to explain his point. "Don't you get it, Val? Once all Seth's yuppie club members taste our wine, they'll want to buy it for their own personal use, as well as recommend it to all their snarky business friends. Before you know it, Heart Winery Wines will be in EVERY upscale home and business in the country! Seth Spencer rubs elbows with some high-class people, you know, and if HE recommends something, it carries clout!" At this point, his eyebrows arched rigidly above his wildly oversized cartoon character eyes, and his forehead was dripping with sweat from his crazed excitement. And like a madman, he kept blabbering on.

"And with the royalties I'll be getting from this brilliant advertising campaign you came up with, I'll finally be able to take that trip to Barossa, as well as introduce Blue Merlot to other worlds! Just THINK of the doors of opportunity THAT could open up for Heart Winery!"

"ROYALTIES? WHAT royalties?" Valli asked in flabbergasted surprise. "Since when do YOU take royalties from one of MY advertising campaigns, Jack?" Stunned, shocked and disgusted, she couldn't believe what she had just heard spew from Jack's greedy lips. She knew he was a shrewd businessman, but he was paid a handsome salary and the talk of "royalties" from ANYTHING had NEVER even come up before now!

Jack slowly walked over and stood directly in front of her. The devilish smirk on his face spoke volumes. For the first time, she was seeing in Jack Conova what she had suspected for years. Greed. Pure, unadulterated GREED.

"Well, well, well now, MISS Heart," he sneered, "You seem to have become quite greedy since your father died. And quite dishonest, I might add. You know FULL WELL that *"we put our heart and soul into every bottle of wine we make"* was MY slogan, and I expect - NO, I DEMAND to be compensated for you using it in your presentation without discussing it with me first!" His tone was harsh, insolent, and condescending, and Valli still couldn't believe what she was hearing.

"Wait just a minute now, Jack ... "she rebutted. But Jack cut her short.

"NO – YOU wait, Valli! I've worked my tail off to get Heart Winery up to this level, and it's because of MY slogan that we got the Crescent Beach Yachtsman Club deal! I'll be damned if I'm going to let YOU or anyone else rob me of what is rightfully mine!" he huffed.

Realizing he was now practically shouting in her face, he backed away, rubbed his hair back with his hands and let out a half-hearted sigh. He needed to get his emotions under control, or he could blow everything. After a few seconds of silence, he turned back to Valli and offered her a reassuring smile.

"Now, look, Val - it's like I said - this is a "win-win" for everyone involved. We're ALL going to make a lot of money from this deal – YOU included, as long as..." It was Valli who cut Jack off this time. She knew EXACTLY where he was going with THOSE words!

"As long as WHAT? As long as, I give you what you want? That IS what you were going to say, isn't it, Jack? I'm not stupid, you know! This isn't about royalties or getting rich, or even compensation - this is about REVENGE! You've finally found a way to hold that little "incident" between us over my head, and if I' don't give you what you want, you'll expose everything, right? That IS what you're REALLY saying, isn't it Jack? This is nothing more than BLACKMAIL!" she seethed.

"Now, Val, sweetheart, don't get alarmed. Blackmail is such a STRONG word. I prefer to think of it as a little "payback". You're just going to pay me back for keeping your little secret, and no one is going to be the wiser."

It was all Valli could do to keep from slapping that arrogant smirk off Jack's face once again! How DARE he do this to her after all her daddy had done for him! She KNEW he always had an angle, but she didn't think he'd stoop so low as to blackmail her! She thought they had agreed to put THAT incident in the PAST, and in fact, she had it tightly corked in her "secret bottle", with all the rest of her unspeakable sins. She couldn't afford any kind of careless leak now - or EVER! But Jack had her between a rock and a hard place, and he knew it! He could really cause her world to come crashing down in a heartbeat if he made good on his backstabbing threat!

Valli felt defeated and ashamed. After all, if it weren't for that little "indiscretion" Jack was about to expose, her father's company - nor her reputation would be in jeopardy right now. But it was MORE than just a little indiscretion - it was a sin that she knew eventually would come back to haunt her one day.

And today was that day.

Not even God could get her out of THIS mess, so she prayed He would at least forgive her for caving in to Jack's spiteful threats!

Chapter 4

"Fine, Jack – you win. How much do you want? What's it going to cost to make you keep your mouth shut?" she finally relented, knowing she had no choice but to cut a deal with him. She could only imagine the outrageous amount he was about to propose, as well as the raised eyebrows of her Board of Directors when she told them why she needed such an exorbitant amount of money. But instead of "taking her to the cleaners", he shocked and surprised her by doing a complete one-eighty.

"No Val," he slowly backed off. "I think I've changed my mind. I don't think I want royalties after all. You're absolutely right, that ISN'T what this is all about."

Whew!

Valli secretly sighed in relief, thankful he saw the ludicrousness of his request. But Jack wasn't through bargaining; he just upped the ante. Another evil grin crossed his lips. More flames danced in his eyes. Satan himself couldn't have been more calculating at that very moment!

"No, no, I think I'd rather have something more impressive; something of a little MORE value. Something with a little more clout. Say like, EQUAL partnership in Heart Winery? Yes – yes, that would be MUCH better, don't you think? A fifty percent stake in Heart Winery! How about it, sweetheart? Ready to make old Jack here your equal partner? We either share in Heart Winery's good fortune from now on, or your dirty little secret makes it way to the front page of the Crescent Beach newspaper!"

His threat dripped with her blood.

Valli's face grew chili pepper red with anger. She stared vehemently at Jack, and was certain Satan was smiling back at her. She blew out a hot breath of air and a few strands of hair fell back across her face. Jack reached over toward her and lightly brushed the hair back from her face. His touch disgusted her, and she quickly slapped his hand away, remembering another time when a dirty hand reached out for her.

"Don't you dare touch me - you greedy bastard!" she spewed back at him. Jack backed away and laughed.

"Easy there, Val. Don't make this so hard, sweetheart. Would it be THAT bad being my equal partner?"

"NO! Absolutely NOT! I promised my father I would NOT let anyone else run this company, and that includes YOU, Jack! I'll give you the damn royalties, but it will be a cold day in hell before I give you equal partnership in Heart Winery!"

Her stance was rock solid as she stood her ground, even though she felt like she was coming unglued inside. She glared back at Jack in cold defiance, knowing she had everything to lose, right down to her palatial office view. Still, she could not let her father down, not even to save herself. It was bad enough she had to live the nightmare of what her mother caused twenty-five years ago; she was NOT going to let Jack degrade and humiliate her by blackmailing her with another shameful indiscretion. She hoped by standing her ground, she could call his bluff and make him reconsider his preposterous request. However, Jack was a tough negotiator, and not about to give in that easily. He folded his arms in lawyer-like rebuttal.

"Well now, isn't that sweet - the way you want to honor your father's memory by upholding his last wishes. That's SO touching." His words were callously cruel and sarcastic.

"I really admire your loyalty, Val, but I HIGHLY suggest you reconsider your decision before tonight's dinner at the Crescent Beach Yachtsman Club – unless you want Seth Spencer, AND the entire club to know your dirty little secret, my dear. No, I'm afraid the subject is NOT open for discussion," he jabbed back.

Nope, just as she suspected, Jack Conova wasn't caving in one little bit. She decided to change tactics and appeal to his conscious, not sure he even had one. She forced a sour lemon smile and held back spit-fire.

"You wouldn't DARE! How could you do this to me, Jack – OR my father, after all he did for you? Doesn't his memory mean ANYTHING to you? He thought of you like a son and gave you a golden opportunity to spread your wings here at Heart Winery to be able to develop all kinds of wines. If not for him, you wouldn't have your little pinky in Heart wines, much less your precious "heart and soul". You should be GRATEFUL to even have a JOB here! And all this because of some silly advertising slogan?"

She thought about turning on the water works, but Jack wasn't the pitying type. She went for the "designing female charm" instead, which she was SURE Jack couldn't resist. She casually pulled her silky blouse down a little lower over her hips, gently twirled her naturally wavy blonde locks between her fingers, and licked her dry, parched lips, all the while staring him down with her come-hither blue eyes.

"Look, Jack, how about if I just pay you a generous royalty for the slogan, and let's move on? I'm willing to negotiate on a reasonable amount. Let's just talk about it!" She smiled a half-naked smile. But Jack wasn't fooled by her Jezebel charms.

The brazen, stone-cold look on his face told her she was losing ground fast, and she was starting to really panic, but couldn't afford to let him know that. She had to remain calm and in control. Still, he was stubborn as the jack-ass he was and didn't budge at all. He just shook his head defiantly back and forth, like a stupid bobble-headed toy.

"Sorry, Val – no deal, babe. It's either an equal partnership or nothing. Stop trying to worm your way out of this. Begging doesn't become you, sweetheart. Besides, would it be all THAT bad – my being your partner? Think of all the fun we could have traveling around the world selling Heart wines – AND all the money we could make together! I could take you places and show you things you've NEVER seen before! Your life would be ten times MORE exciting than it is now, my dear!"

He neared closer and once again lightly brushed her cheek with the back of his hand but didn't say a word. His haunting brown eyes and Casanova charm was almost enough to melt her thorny resolve. She felt her knees go as weak and wobbly as a baby bird. Why did he have to be so DAMN good looking? She had always been a sucker for a handsome man and a smooth talker. He slowly backed away, picked up his briefcase and headed for the door, but not before leaving her with a few last words.

"You think about it, Val, but I'll expect your answer by eight o clock tonight; otherwise, I'm afraid it's going to be a VERY uncomfortable dinner for everyone – especially YOU! See you at the club, sweetheart!"

He slowly sauntered out of the conference room, his cocky ego boldly following behind. Valli buried her burning face in her hands and softly wept. The monkey on her back now felt like a five-hundred-pound gorilla, and she wished her daddy were still there to take her in his arms and tell her everything was going to be alright. Instead, she silently cried out to God, hoping He wasn't too busy to hear her pitiful pleas one more time.

Needing to get away from Jack's dark, lingering presence, she retreated to her ocean office paradise to contemplate the daunting decision before her. He had caught her totally off guard and she was still stunned by his insidious request. How long had he been harboring this corrupt scheme to take over Heart Winery? How could she have been so blind to his ulterior motives? There were plenty of unanswered questions, but unfortunately, no time to ponder answers. Jack expected an answer by eight, and there was only one acceptable answer in his eyes – to become her partner and stock owner in fifty percent of Heart Winery. After that, it would just be a matter of time before he started running things HIS way, possibly forcing her OUT, and taking FULL control! She just couldn't let that happen, but there seemed to be no easy alternative. Jack was determined to blackmail her if she didn't come through and tell the world her ugly secret. The very thought made her ghastly nauseous.

She finally decided there was nothing left to do but go along with him and try to retain as much control of the company as possible. It still wouldn't guarantee her that Jack wouldn't still threaten to expose her if she went against him again. But if she gave in, she would always be a slave to his threats; and if she refused to give in, he could ruin her AND everything her father worked so hard for. She felt trapped by her ill-fated choices, and ashamed of the shameful secret that Jack was hanging over her head. She gazed out the window at the glorious ocean view in front of her and bowed her head.

"Lord, I feel so alone right now, and don't know which way to turn. I'm torn between honoring my father's wishes, and selfishly protecting my own pitiful reputation. I've never been good at making decisions on my own, as I always seem to make the wrong ones. I'm asking you now to help me make the RIGHT decision and give me the courage to face the consequences of either. Amen."

She waited for a divine reassurance of peace to wash over her, but her mind and body were just as anxious-ridden as ever. She knew in her heart what she must do and was already dreading the outcome of the only obvious decision she could make. She could only hope God would at least give her the grace to handle it in a way that would make her father proud.

Needing to clear her head, she decided to take the rest of the day off and spend it perusing the Crescent Beach waterfront. Maybe the fresh salt air and diverse scenery would prepare her for the dubious task that lie ahead. She would need to plan her words carefully and be in strong mental shape to face Jack later that evening. She made a quick phone call, closed her office and headed back home to change clothes before heading out to the waterfront.

Meanwhile, back at Heart Winery, Jack was already planning his "celebratory promotion" speech, and eventual takeover of Heart Winery.

"Now, you must act VERY surprised when you hear Valli make the announcement that she is bringing me on as a partner – AND make sure you congratulate HER on making such a "wise" decision!" he instructed Seth Spencer, who had merely slipped out of sight until Valli had left the building, and then returned.

"What makes you so SURE Valli is going to go along with you on this, Jack?"

"Because Valli Heart isn't going to risk her precious reputation, or take a chance on losing her father's estate," he smugly answered. "She absolutely has NO other choice but to make me partner, and she knows it! That "incident" between us pretty much sealed the deal – and my future as OWNER of this winery one day! We couldn't have planned it out any better, my friend, and now we're BOTH going to reap the rewards! Here's to US, Seth!" he cheered, raising his wine glass to Seth's.

Hideous laughter filled the room as he and Seth Spencer clanked their wine glasses together and toasted to Jack's upcoming "promotion". The rest of the evening would be an academy award performance with the Oscar going to Jack and Seth for the brilliant and hostile takeover of Heart Winery.

Chapter 5

After wandering around the waterfront for what seemed like hours, Valli found herself standing on the mostly deserted dock, save for a few lonely fishermen coming in for the day. How she wished she could just jump on one of those boats, and sail ten thousand miles out to sea. She didn't care where – just somewhere far away from all the weighty cares and constant struggles she faced. Oftentimes, she even wished she'd had a brother that her father could have groomed to take over Heart Winery, instead of handing it down to her. Then she could just hide away in her office all day, and design brilliant advertising campaigns instead of jumping through corporate hoops with the likes of Jack Conova. But with her father gone, she felt even more alone and inept to make even simple day to day decisions and realized she had relied on Jack way too often to make those decisions for her. Decisions she should have been making herself, like her father did. How ashamed he would be of her now to see how she'd let Jack blackmail her into possibly losing the only heritage he had to leave his only child.

She felt like such a fool for trusting Jack so much, especially now, knowing how ruthless he could be. She couldn't stop thinking about his double crossing "demand" to make him equal partners with her. The egotistical, sanctimonious devil!

Anger arose in her like a fierce nor'easter. She felt the cold blood in her veins rise to the boiling point. She watched as a fisherman mercilessly gutted a large sea trout with a sharp serrated scaling knife, and maliciously imagined it was Jack's blood splattering all over the pristine white sides of the boat. Even though she knew murder was a sin, she was SO angry with Jack, she was sure if given a knife or a gun, she could kill him – just like the LAST man that tried to hurt her. As she watched the fisherman steadfastly slaughter his day's catch, her mind drifted back to that dark and formidable night...

She was only eighteen. Not quite a woman, and still very much a child. Yet despite her immature mind, her young, still-virgin body was quickly blossoming into that of a desirable young woman, voluptuous in all the right places, and an irresistible pleasure for dirty old men. Especially the dirty old men her mother had occasion to pick up whenever her father was out of town. It was one of those precise times that her mother went down to the local bar, found herself a cheap drunk and promptly invited him home. Valli was stretched out on the couch in cut-off denim shorts and a skimpy halter top watching TV when they came shamelessly stumbling in. She could still recall the drunken, boisterous laughter outside the front door, and smell the soured odor of cheap alcohol on their breaths.

"Aw, c'mon baby cakes – how's about another kissy-kissy for your fella?" her mother's drunken visitor begged with a slurred tongue.

"Shh, honey – my daughter might be asleep – you'll waky her uppy! We has to be ver-rrry quiet," she giggled back.

"Too late, Mom – I'm still awake," Valli called out from the den. She jumped up from the couch and ran to the front door to try and keep the unwelcome visitor from coming in any further.

"Who's your drunk friend, and don't you think you need to call him a cab home?" she questioned her mother.

"Oh, hello baby girl. This is .... what'd ya say your name was again, honey – Sam?" she asked, pushing Valli aside and stumbling over to the wine bar.

"Hell, whatever you WANT it to be, baby cakes!" the drunken man blabbered in response, quickly following behind her.

"MOTHER!" Valli sharply scolded. "How dare you bring another man in this house with Daddy gone – don't you have any respect for your own husband – and MY father?"

"Oh, don't be such a baby, Valli – me and Sam here are just friends – ain't that right Sammy, honey?"

She pulled the cork stopper from a bottle of wine and took a hard swig, then handed the bottle to Sam, who promptly turned it up and drank like a thirsty camel, then passed it back to her mother. They continued this back and forth ritual for several minutes, sloshing wine everywhere from their clothes to the carpeted floor below. Valli grew more and more disgusted with her mother's unacceptable behavior and begged her to send her drunken friend home.

"Mother, PLEASE get that wasted scumbag out of here and go to bed before you do something stupid!" Her mother's inebriated friend didn't take too kindly to her rude invitation to leave.

"Well, now, pretty little girl – maybe YOU'RE the one who needs to go to bed. Isn't it past your beddy-bye time?" Sam bellowed. "Maybe you'd like Uncle Sam help you into your jammies and tuck you in!" he slobbered, stumbling closer to Valli, and reaching out to her with his grubby hands.

"Get away from me, you old drunken pervert!" Valli yelled, backing away from him and moving towards her father's big oak desk. Sam kept coming at her, his map-lined bloodshot eyes undressing her with every step.

"Oh, so you playing hard to get with old Sam now, huh? Well maybe I need to teach you some respect for your elders!" he angrily replied. He started to loosen his belt buckle and moved in even closer to Valli. Her mother, in a raging jealous fit, stumbled over and tried to get between them.

"Oh, Sam – leave her alone – she ain't nothin' but a young-un! I'm a REAL woman – you can help me take my clothes off!" she teased, trying to lure him away from Valli.

"Get away from me old woman – can't you see this smart-alecky little girl needs a good whipping before she goes to bed?" he yelled, pushing her mother to the floor, and tripping over a recliner in the process, sending him promptly to the floor, as well.

As Sam scrambled to pick himself up off the floor, Valli immediately took the opportunity to grab her father's .38 revolver from the nearby desk, jumped up on the couch and pointed the gun in Sam's direction. Finally getting to his feet, he once again stumbled toward her, totally oblivious to the loaded barrel of a gun staring back.

"Now you're REALLY going to get it, you little tease!" Sam threatened, still groping his way toward Valli.

"STOP right there or I'll shoot!" Valli warned him. "I mean it, don't come any closer!" she screamed.

Her poignant warning, however, fell on deaf, drunken ears as Sam lunged forward and groped for her over-developed teenage breasts. She knew she had no choice but to defend herself against this drunken lunatic. She slowly cocked the hammer back, her untrained finger shaking nervously against the trigger. She shut her eyes tight to the cataclysmic horror to come.

"NO! Valli, NO – DON'T!" her mother screamed, begging Valli not to shoot the rapist before her. But it was too late. Valli felt her finger release the trigger as Sam's bloodshot eyes widened in horror.

BANG!

The gun shot was deafening, and the next sound she remembered was Sam hitting the floor with a loud thud.

A nearby neighbor heard the gunshot and called the police. When they arrived, Valli was found huddled in the corner of the room sobbing and shaking, and her mother laying crumpled up beside Sam, who had died from a single gunshot wound to the chest.

Her father was summoned home from his business trip, and the family attorney was appointed to defend Valli in court. It was a swift trial, and Valli was found not guilty of murder by reason of self-defense, upheld by her mother's testimony and admission of adultery with another man.

Things were never the same between her mother and father afterwards, and they eventually divorced. Valli and her father moved to another house and although she never again spoke about the incident with anyone, the ghosts and demons of that fateful night remained with her - determined to haunt her the rest of her life.

When she found out her mother was dying of cancer years later, she finally made peace with her, but the horrid memories still lingered. And even though she was exonerated from any wrong-doing, she always felt somehow guilty – like it was all HER fault. Insurmountable guilt that continued to haunt her and tarnish every relationship she tried to have with a man. Now Jack was about to bring yet another shameful incident to light unless…. Her secret thoughts quickly trailed off as a voice behind her broke in.

"I'm sorry I'm late, baby – thought I'd NEVER get away from him!" Finally – the calming and familiar voice she had so patiently waited for!

"Oh Seth, darling - thank God – I thought you'd never get here!" She buried her face in Seth Spencer's broad chest and fell into the strong arms of his loving embrace.

"How'd things go with Jack after I left?" she lightly whispered to him. Seth caressed her hair and whispered back, "Perfect, darling. I've got him eating out of my hand! You just keep on playing your part, and we'll lure him right into our trap!"

"Oh, Seth - I'm SO ready for all this to be over with! How much LONGER do I have to go on pretending?"

"Not much longer, sweetheart - not much longer at all…."

Chapter 6

Valli had met Seth Spencer at a Young Christian Singles Club event just a year ago. She had been trying to get out more and mingle with "the right kind of people" but found most of them at the YCSC to be too caught up in their religion and even self-righteous. Except Seth. Seth was different. Although he "came from money", he never put on airs around her or made her feel unworthy of his attentions, nor did he judge her for her past sins. He was also genuinely kind, easy-going and always the perfect gentleman.

As their platonic friendship grew into a more serious relationship, they started seeing each other outside the YCSC on a more "romantic basis". Knowing the other "highly conservative" members of the YCSC would disapprove of their "sinful" lifestyle, they both left the group and would rendezvous quite frequently on one of Seth's five private yachts for long, romantic nights of exotic dinners and passionate lovemaking. Sometimes, Seth would carry her to a private island about thirty miles north of Crescent Beach, where they would spend the day lounging on the deserted beach or visiting the quaint little island shops. And planning their future. A future not only to be together forever, but to eventually run Heart Winery together - WITHOUT Jack Conova!

Valli was crazy in love with Seth, and their clandestine plan to get the proprietary secret recipe to Jack's Blue Merlot, and then give him the boot, was too well thought out and precise for there to be any slip-ups now. They were SO close, and if their plan succeeded, Seth would join her as a TRUE equal partner, Heart Winery would attain global notoriety, and she would become the VERY RICH Mrs. Seth Spencer! If she could just hold on a little longer, she would finally have everything she ever wanted! And even though her past "secret indiscretions" constantly nagged at her, she convinced herself it was what God wanted for her.

Back at his private yacht, Seth poured Valli a glass of an expensive imported Italian red wine. "Here darling, you look like you could use this." Valli took a long, slow deliberate swallow and breathed out a draining sigh.

"Mm... this is SO good - you're right, darling, I definitely needed that! In fact, after today, I think I could drink the whole bottle!" she dryly joked. After another sip, she sat her wine glass down and turned away from Seth. Her face was wrought with worry, and he knew her well enough to know when something was wrong.

"What is it, Val? What's wrong, darling?"

"I'm worried Seth. Are you SURE we're doing the right thing - tricking Jack like this? I mean after all, without him, I'm not sure Heart Winery would be where it is today! And you know how much my father thought of him. Isn't there another way to make him give us that recipe?"

Seth held Valli's face gently in his hands and tenderly kissed her lips. His kiss was like a soothing balm, instantly easing every tense muscle in her body.

"Valli, sweetheart, I understand how you feel, but you can't go soft on me now. You don't owe Jack Conova anything! Are you forgetting the impossible situation he's putting you in already? Why would you even WANT someone like that working at Heart Winery? And I'm sure if your father knew how he was now, he wouldn't want him there either! He would have gotten rid of him a LONG time ago! Besides, darling, you don't give yourself enough credit. YOU are the marketing genius behind Heart Winery, and I have just as much knowledge of the wine industry as Jack. He's not the ONLY one who studied Oenology, remember!"

It was true. Seth had a degree from Sonoma State University in California, and "wineology" was a second language for him. It's one reason he befriended Jack a few years earlier - in hopes of eventually partnering with him in the business. Only Jack had his own selfish agenda. When Seth realized what Jack's plans were, he conspired with Valli to get the Blue Merlot recipe and give Jack the boot. Seth knew from the first moment he tasted Blue Merlot, how special it was, and how it would be sought out by fine wine connoisseurs all over the world. But it was a proprietary blend, and ONLY Jack knew the recipe.

"Now all we need is that special Blue Merlot recipe, and together we can run Heart Winery even better WITHOUT Jack! I thought that's what you wanted!"

"Oh, Seth, you know it is. I guess my conscience is just working a little overtime. And no, I haven't forgotten the stunt he's trying to pull! You're so right – he has all this coming to him, and if anything, he OWES me that recipe for Blue Merlot. If my father hadn't given him a job at Heart Winery, he might not ever have had the opportunity to develop it. Heart Winery gave him a chance to make it in this industry and he used that opportunity to take advantage of my father AND me! You're right - I don't owe him ANYTHING, and that Blue Merlot recipe belongs to ME and my father's company. I guess I just hate we have to go to such lengths to get it from him!"

"Well, if he hadn't been so selfish in wanting to keep it to himself, we might not HAVE to go to such lengths. But don't forget, baby, it has been Jack's plans all along to get rid of YOU and take over Heart Winery. If he hadn't confessed that to me, YOU might be the one getting the boot! Now stop worrying! Our plan is rock solid and in just a few more weeks, we'll be celebrating in some romantic tropical island – over a big prized bottle of Blue Merlot! Please, just promise me you'll hang in there a little longer?"

It all made perfect sense when Seth spelled it out. Still, Valli wasn't brought up to be so manipulative or conniving. And even though she knew what Jack wanted to do was wrong, she just didn't feel right in her heart about the plans she had made with Seth. She was sure the Bible said something about not "plotting evil thoughts in your heart about others", but she just figured she was "righting a wrong" that Jack was doing.

"Vengeance is mine, so saith the Lord," also came to mind, but she couldn't take a chance on waiting for the Lord to bring vengeance quick enough! If Jack got enough dollar signs in his eyes and decided to

sell that prized recipe to another winery, it could be curtains for Heart Winery - and her!

Besides, she trusted Seth, and knew he would never do anything to hurt her or Heart Winery. Her whole future was depending on their plan and she hoped God would forgive her if she was doing anything wrong Valli gazed confidently into Seth's reassuring eyes and saw her future gleaming brighter than ever. Even the demons that usually interrupted her sacred dreams couldn't dishearten her hopes now. She grabbed his hands and wrapped them tightly around hers.

"Yes, darling - I'll hold on - for as LONG as you say! You just watch me tonight! I'll put on the BEST Oscar winning performance you've ever seen!" Her blue eyes danced and sparkled at the thought of making Seth proud of her.

He pulled her closer, and gently kissed her forehead. "That's my girl! Tonight's a VERY important night and we've BOTH got to put on our best performances if we're going to even have a shot at getting Jack to give up that secret Blue Merlot recipe! Once he thinks he's got you OUT, he'll bring ME on board as his partner, and share that secret recipe with me. After that, we'll turn the tables on HIM, and he'll be history!"

"Oh, Seth, darling, your plan is simply brilliant, and I just KNOW it's going to work! You're not only the most sexy and successful man I've ever known, you're also the smartest!" she cooed sweetly in his ear.

Seth once again cupped her blushing cheeks in his strong hands. His touch was gentle, warm and arousing. She closed her eyes and waited for the powerful magnetic force that would magically draw their lips closer together. Seth didn't linger. Within seconds, she was swept away to a dreamy fantasy land, where her mind and body were free to play and wander in the lustful fields of love and romance. His kisses were more intoxicating than the fine wine she had sipped earlier, and she felt her body longing to melt like hot candle wax beneath his.

But all too quickly, the kiss was over, as Seth withdrew his lips, and her fantasy quickly faded like watercolors in the summer rain.

"You better hurry home and get ready for tonight, darling," he coaxed. "And wear that pretty blue ruffled dress – it goes so well with your beautiful baby blue eyes!"

"Aw, I'd rather stay here with you, baby – and wear NOTHING," Valli teased.

"So would I darling, but we've got this one last scene to play out. Then I promise you there will be endless nights of love and romance in the most romantic places in the world! How does that sound?"

"Heavenly," Valli contently sighed. "Just heavenly" ...

Chapter 7

While getting ready for the big celebration, Valli couldn't stop thinking about Jack's REAL intentions, and how he used her all along to get what he wanted. And even though Seth assured her their plan was "iron-clad", she worried Jack might still expose their "dirty little secret" to the world – especially after he got the boot from Heart Winery! It's not like he had a lot to lose at that point, and hell hath no fury like a scorned "Jack"! She fretted and worried about the possible "what ifs."

Like, what if he turned the tables back on her and caused a public scandal? She could always deny everything, and say he was just trying to get even with her for letting him go, but she still risked the chance it could get real ugly - real FAST. The repercussions on Heart Winery could be devastating! And even with Jack gone, the risk of scandal WOULDN'T be, despite Seth's assurance of a rosy future. No, it was still a risk she just wasn't sure she was willing to take.

She paced back and forth nervously, pondering her few options. After much justifiable deliberation, she finally decided there was only ONE sure fire way to make sure Jack didn't talk, and she couldn't believe she was even considering such a drastic measure! She looked at her watch. It would soon be time to meet Jack and Seth at the Yacht Club, and she knew Jack would be expecting her answer. She quickly dialed his number on her cell phone.

"Well, well, l thought I might be hearing from you about now, Val." His tone was cold and smug.

"I've got to see you before we go to the Yacht Club, Jack. Meet me in my office in thirty minutes."

"I hope you're not playing games with me, Valli. You know there's only one thing I want to hear from you, so you better not be wasting my time."

"You'll get what you want, Jack. I just need a little extra "insurance" to make sure you keep your promise."

"You're really not in any position to bargain with ME, Valli, since I'm the one holding all the cards in this little game, but just to amuse you, I'll meet you there. Don't be late – we DO have a celebration dinner at eight, remember?" He laughed an ugly, vindictive laugh as the phone line went dead.

Valli pulled open the dresser drawer and reached to the far back. Her fingers felt the smooth, cold tip barrel of a .38 revolver. She really didn't want a gun, but her father bought her one after that dreadful night she gunned down her drunken attacker, and insisted she keep it for her own protection. She hadn't touched a gun since then, and she didn't want to use one now, but Jack left her with no other choice. She was not about to let another man hurt her – OR steal her father's company from her.

Besides, Jack had given her the perfect alibi – the "threat". All she had to say was that she met with him to "work out something", but he refused to negotiate, got mad and violent, and tried to physically attack her. It would be another perfect case of self-defense, but with no witnesses. Just her word against his. It was the ONLY way to get rid of Jack - and his threats once and for all.

We'll see who has the last laugh now, Jack Conova. It'll be the LAST time you laugh!

She found the box of bullets in the same drawer, quickly loaded the gun and placed it in her purse.

THOU SHALT NOT KILL!

The strict Biblical commandment pounded in her head like a mighty clap of thunder from heaven. The thought was so strong, she felt her knees go weak, and nearly fell to the bedroom floor. What was she thinking? She couldn't possibly kill another man – not even one as back-stabbing and conniving as Jack Conova!

She glanced up and caught a shameful reflection of herself in the dresser mirror. Deep-creased wrinkles around her eyes and mouth reflected years of pain and worry. Her sallow skin was cracked and dry. Her once sapphire blue eyes were now a faded shade of gray and riddled with squiggly red lines. Dark, puffy bags sat just beneath her bottom lids, and seemed to carry the weight of her soul within them. As hard as she had tried to rise above all the misery the world had dished out to her, it never seemed to stop. A woman could only take so much, and as for Valli, well, she was at her breaking point. She had been pushed to the limit and it was getting harder and harder to fight back.

THOU SHALT NOT KILL!

The mighty words of God spoke to her again – only this time they were strangely calm, as if God were saying, *I know how you feel, but this isn't the way to handle things. Trust me to work it out a better way. I will never leave you or forsake you. Trust ME, Valli.*

Valli fell back on the bed and dropped her head in shame. She knew what she was about to do was not just wrong – but illegal, as well. She was about to sin against God and break the law. Satan had cleverly and quietly misled her down a wicked path of lies, deception and now almost murder! Big drops of sweat beaded around her forehead, and her hands were sopping wet and clammy. She dropped to the floor on her knees and begged God to forgive her for the sinful thoughts in her mind. She cried out to the only One who could make things right.

She wept softly for the young eighteen-year-old girl whose own mother almost allowed a drunken slob to almost savagely rape her only daughter. She wept for the loss of the only man who had never let her down – her father. She wept for the shameful transgression she had with Jack. She wept for what seemed like hours, until she was drained of tears and numb from grief.

Knowing she didn't have long before she was to meet Jack, she picked herself up off the floor from her crumpled state, brushed the wrinkles from her clothes, and freshened her hair and makeup. She knew now what she must do. She just hoped God would give her the strength to do it and forgive her for it at the same time.

Chapter 8

Jack's car was already in the parking lot when Valli arrived at her office complex.

Figures he'd be early; probably wants a little extra time to gloat! She pulled up a few parks away from him, but noticed he wasn't in his car. She figured he must be waiting in the reception area outside her office, as she kept her office locked and he didn't have a key. At least she didn't THINK he did.

Walking through the front door of the building, she began to feel very nervous about what she was getting ready to do. She flipped the light switch at the bottom of the stairs, to light her way up the darkened stairs to her upstairs office. How odd, she thought, that Jack hadn't turned the lights on himself. As she rounded the corner at the top of the stairs, she noticed the door to her office was slightly ajar, and the room eerily dark. She called out nervously into the black darkness.

"Jack, are you here?" There was no answer.

She slowly pushed the door open a little further, reached over to the wall, flipped on the switch, and stretched her neck out just enough to peek in. A blood curdling scream pounded in her head, and it took a minute for her to realize it was her own! Blinking her eyes several times in disbelief, she was frozen at the gory sight before her. A blood-covered man laid motionless on the carpeted floor of her office.

It was Jack!

Disregarding any unknown dangers still lurking around, she quickly ran over and knelt beside him, lifted his arm and felt his wrist for a pulse. Nothing. She bent over his chest to listen for a heartbeat. Still nothing.

Jack Conova was DEAD!

Dark crimson blood oozed from a large open wound in his chest and puddled around his body from an obvious bullet wound to his heart. Not only was he dead, he apparently had been MURDERED!

Finally realizing the imminent danger she could be in, she looked cautiously around to see if the attacker was still around, but apparently, they had already fled the scene. She raced to the phone on her desk, and quickly dialed 911.

"Yes, I'd like to report a murder!" she cried out to the emergency dispatcher. The battery of questions that followed irritated and confused her.

"How do I KNOW he was murdered? Well, it's kind of obvious when there's a big hole in his chest and blood is going everywhere!" she sarcastically replied.

"Suicide? Are you kidding me? NO – Jack would have NEVER killed himself – I can assure you of that!"

"Murder weapon? No, I don't SEE a gun or anything lying around; I'm assuming they took that with them! Would you like me to go out and look for it while the murderer is catching a ride out of town?" She was getting more and more disgusted with the seemingly senseless questions. Why didn't they stop wasting time, and just send someone over right away?

Finally, after a few more questions, the dispatcher told her to stay put, and that someone would be there shortly. While she waited for the police and ambulance to arrive, she had plenty questions of her own to ponder:

How did this happen? Did Jack interrupt a robber, and get shot in the getaway? If so, WHO could it have been, and WHAT could they possibly be looking for in HER office? She had no valuables or money stowed away there – only marketing files and documents. No, a robbery gone bad was NOT likely the motive here!

There had to be another reason. It had to be someone who KNEW Jack and WANTED him dead! Someone who MUST have known Jack was coming to meet her and got there first. A sickening thought came to mind. There was only ONE other person who could have known about her plans, and who would have had just as much reason to want Jack dead as much as she did. She shut her eyes tight, to try and force the awful thought from her mind. But it didn't work. It was the only obvious answer.

Seth. It HAD to have been Seth. The nauseating thought made her feel like a thousand maggots were eating away at her stomach.

Why, Seth? Why??

She tried to reason it all out in her head. Jack must have called Seth right after he hung up talking to her, told him he was meeting her there, and maybe even confessed his plans to kill her! Seth's yacht club was closer, so he must have gotten there first, waited for Jack in her darkened office, then shot him when he came in. Seth must have then slipped out and got out of sight right before she got there.

She looked around again for the murder weapon, but there was no gun lying around. She knew Seth had a trophy case of prized guns on his private yacht, and he could have used any one of them. But Seth was a smart man, and surely wouldn't have used his own registered gun, nor would he have left any obvious clues that would have led authorities to suspect he was the killer. And without a witness or tangible evidence, they would never be able to tie him to the murder of Jack Conova. It was the perfect murder - as long as they didn't know about her and Seth's plans to get rid of Jack. Plans NO ONE could EVER know!

She knew they both would be heavily interrogated, and it was even MORE critical now than ever before that they keep up their "act". She HAD to talk to Seth before the authorities got there. She quickly dialed his cell phone, and nervously tapped her nails on the desk while waiting for him to answer. Three rings went by and he still hadn't answered.

"Damnit, Seth, answer your phone!" she muttered impatiently under her breath.

"Val, hello darling! Couldn't wait to talk to me at the Club tonight?" he teased after finally answering.

"Seth, hush and listen! I don't have much time. I just got to my office, and I know what you did to Jack! But don't worry, darling – I won't say anything about our plans or US. I'll keep our little secret tighter than Fort Knox!" The words continued to spill haphazardly from her lips, as she kept a diligent watch out her office window for the police.

"I should have known Jack would call you to let you know I wanted to meet him. I know I should have called you and told you, but I thought I could handle him on my own. I'm so sorry you got all caught up in all this, sweetheart!"

Confused with her foolish blabbering, Seth finally cut in and pressed for more details. "Valli, baby, calm down and tell me what on earth you're talking about?! Where are you, and what has happened to Jack?"

It suddenly occurred to Valli that she may have screwed things up by calling Seth. Of course, he had to "play dumb" – in case the police subpoenaed their phone records. Surely it wouldn't look good to see that she placed a call to her lover right after finding Jack dead! She pretended to play along.

"Never mind, darling. We can talk later. I'm at my office, and Jack Conova has been murdered! I've already called 911, and the police are on the way. Oh, Seth, I'm so scared. Who could have done this to him?"

"What?! Jack's DEAD? And you think I did it?" Seth shouted in horror. "Valli, I didn't kill Jack! Why on earth would you think THAT?"

"But I just assumed you…,"

The absurdity of her words stopped her from continuing, not to mention her bewilderment over Seth's immediate denial.

"Never mind, just listen to me." His instructions were explicit, and Valli strained over the receiver to make sure she understood.

"I'm calling my attorney right now and we'll meet you there. Whatever you do, do NOT talk to the police! Wait for us to get there, understand?"

"Yes, of course, but why don't you want ME to talk to the police? I've got nothing to hide. I'm the one that found his body for Heaven's sake! You don't think they would consider ME as a suspect, do you?"

"Well, Jack DID try to blackmail you into making him a partner at Heart Winery, remember? You've got more of a motive, than I do! Just don't say anything until we get there, okay? I love you, baby!"

"Okay, Seth, whatever you say. I love you, too, darling. I'll be right here. But please hurry!"

Even though Seth told her not to talk, she knew she would look guilty if she refused to talk. She quickly rehearsed in her head what she would say when the police questioned about her reason for wanting to meet Jack in her office. She thought for a minute, then an idea hit her. She would just go along with Jack's plan and say she had decided to make him a partner and had called him to her office to tell him "in private." She'd pretend she was madly in love with him and wanted to "celebrate" with him in her office. She quickly conjured up some fake tears and tried to act shocked and distraught. If ever there was a time to put on an act, this was it. And considering how much she loathed Jack Conova, that was going to be a major performance! She knew they would interrogate Seth, as well, so their stories had to be consistent, AND believable. Seth was the only other one who knew what Jack was trying to do, and surely, he wouldn't confess that to the police. That would be suicide for them both!

Finally, she heard footsteps rushing up the stairs. The police and paramedics had arrived. She quickly flung herself over Jack's lifeless body and sobbed uncontrollably.

"Ms. Heart? I'm Captain Frank Brown, Crescent Beach Police. This is Detective Joe Reuben," he said, pointing to the tall, lanky man beside him. "I know this is a big shock, but we need to speak to you for a few minutes. Your testimony right now could help us apprehend a suspect sooner than later. Can you pull yourself together enough to answer a few questions?"

Captain Brown was a veteran with the Crescent Beach P.D. and reminded Valli of jolly 'ole Saint Nick. His wispy, snowy white hair glistened with streaks of silver was neatly combed to one side, and his amber colored eyes laughed warmly through thin, round silver-rimmed glasses. He spoke with authority, but with the compassion and professionalism of a seasoned police officer, unlike his snotty, bird-legged side-kick, Detective Reuben, who reminded her more of the coarse and nasty Grinch!

Valli nodded, slowly lifted herself up, and walked over to the sofa. Captain Brown followed behind while the paramedics assessed the body, and Detective Rueben scoured the crime scene looking for clues. She answered the Captain's questions through muffled sobs.

"Yes, of course. Just give me a minute or two. This has been such a shock. I just don't know who could have killed poor Jack. He was such a good man. I loved him so much...." Her words trailed off in jerky wails of uncontrollable sobs.

"We're very sorry for your loss, Ms. Heart. So, you know this man?" Valli stared over at Jack's lifeless body and slowly nodded her head up and down. The Captain gently prodded her to continue talking.

"Okay now, just take your time Ms. Heart and tell me what happened." The Captain was genuinely kind and sympathetic, and Valli felt guilty for the bold faced lies she was about to tell.

"Thank you, Captain Brown. I'll try," she sniffed. "You see, Jack works with me at Heart Winery. He's not only a brilliant winemaker, but he was a close friend, as well. VERY close, if you know what I mean." She looked up at the Captain and raised both eyebrows to make her point. Captain Brown nodded in acknowledgement. Valli continued explaining, choosing her words wisely.

"Well, anyway, I had decided to make Jack my equal partner, and called him to meet me here to surprise him. You know, PRIVATELY." More raised eyebrows. Captain Brown nodded again.

"What time did you last speak to Mr. Conova?"

"About six-thirty, I guess. We were supposed to meet here around seven."

"Okay, so what happened when you got here?".

Valli wiped her eyes and sniffled a few more times. "Well, his car was already here, so I came on upstairs. When I got to the top of the stairs, I noticed the door to my office was open, so I went on in and that's when...."

Valli broke down in forced tears once again as she tried to continue with her fabricated story. "I'm really sorry – this is just so...so... hard. I just can't believe he's DEAD!" She dropped her head to her chest and let out a pitiful, gutted moan.

"Okay, Ms. Heart, take it easy. Just a few more questions. Can you tell me if you saw anyone else around, or heard anything suspicious when you arrived?"

"No, no ...there was no one else around. The building was closed, and I guess everyone had left for the day. And no one else has a key to my office, that I know of."

"Not even Mr. Conova?"

"Uh, well, of course, Jack does. I mean, yes, I'm sure I gave him a key," she quickly lied.

"Hey, Captain. Better look at this," Detective Reuben called from the doorway of Valli's office. Captain Brown walked over to the door where the Detective was standing.

"Looks like the door has been jimmied open. Whoever it was, DIDN'T have a key, or either they forgot to bring it!" he sarcastically remarked. The Captain and Detective Reuben both looked at Valli for a response. Valli shot them a surprised look, and a flimsy explanation.

"Of course – that must be it! Someone must have been trying to break into my office when Jack arrived, and he surprised them. They got scared, shot him and ran off right before I got here!" Her story sounded convincing enough, and she was proud of herself for thinking so quickly on her feet. Detective Reuben was not so convinced.

"Uh huh. So, what do you think a crook would be looking for in here, Ms. Heart? Do you have anything of any value here?"

"No, not really, but the crook didn't know that, did he? Maybe he thought I had money or guns in here or something. How am I supposed to know what he was looking for? That's YOUR job, isn't it?" she backhandedly replied.

She turned her attention back toward Jack. A few more fake tears welled up in her eyes and trickled down her cheeks. "I just hate that my poor Jack showed up before I did. I'd rather it been ME that got killed instead of him!" she cried, dropping her head down into her hands.

Captain Brown and Detective Reuben waited patiently, while Valli carried on with her "distraught lover" act. Finally, she lifted herself up and slowly walked over to get a tissue from her purse on the chair where she had laid it when she came in. Clumsily, she knocked her purse off the chair and, it fell on the floor. She watched in horror as the handgun she had put in it earlier, slid out directly in plain view of Captain Brown and the Detective. They both looked at each other with raised eyebrows.

"Well, well, what do we have here? Looks like a gun," Detective Reuben curiously replied. Valli quickly reached down to pick it up, but Detective Reuben stopped her.

"Don't touch the gun, Ms. Heart. I'm afraid we're going to have to check it out since it's at the murder scene."

Valli's face went stark white. She had meant to put the gun back in the drawer before she left home but forgot. Detective Reuben immediately placed in it a plastic evidence bag, he fished from his coat pocket.

"Do you have a permit to carry this gun, Ms. Heart?" Captain Brown asked. Valli stuttered nervously as she strung together a sloppy lie.

"Well, uh, no. I mean, my father gave it to me years ago, you know, for protection. I've never even used it, and I just forgot I even had it in my purse." She laughed weakly, and Detective Reuben and Captain

Brown exchanged doubtful, arched eyebrow-raised glances at her pathetic attempt to cover her lies.

Captain Brown immediately suspected a possible lover's quarrel gone bad. "I'm afraid you're going to have to come down to the station with us, Ms. Heart."

"But, why? I haven't done anything! You have no right to make me go anywhere!" Valli protested.

Before she knew what was happening, Captain Brown twisted her arms behind her back, and slapped a pair of shiny metal handcuffs on her wrists.

"Ms. Heart, you are under arrest for suspicion in the murder of Jack Conova. Anything you say can and will be used against you in a court of law…."

As Valli was being whisked down the stairs to the police car, Seth and his attorney arrived. Seeing Valli being led away in handcuffs, Seth shook his fist and shouted at Captain Brown. "What's going on here, where are you taking her?!"

"Out of the way, sir, you're interfering with police business. Ms. Heart will be at the police station if you wish to meet us there," Captain Brown responded.

"Seth, help me – don't let them do this – PLEASE! Help!" Valli cried as she was escorted to, and promptly shoved in the back of the police car. Seth stood in shock and disbelief as he watched the police car drive away.

What had Valli done? What had she told them? And why were they arresting her? Could it be?! Could SHE be Jack's murderer?

Chapter 9

Back at the police station, Detective Reuben was relentless in his interrogation, and Valli, remembering Seth's instructions to keep quiet, struggled to resist the urge to defend herself against his allegations.

"So, tell me again Ms. Heart – why did you bring a gun with you to meet Jack Conova at your office if you weren't planning to use it?"

Valli tried to stick to her previous lies "I told you. I was meeting Jack to tell him I was making him an equal partner in Heart Winery, and to celebrate in private - if you get my drift, Detective Reuben! I just simply forgot that gun was in my purse! There is NO connection, and I highly resent the implication that you think I am a murderer! Besides, you'll see when the ballistics report comes back that it was NOT the same gun used to kill Jack!"

"But you HAVE killed a man before, haven't you, Ms. Heart?" the Detective asked in a scathing tone.

His jagged question stabbed at Valli with piercing memories of the nightmare she still couldn't forget. Apparently, neither had Detective Reuben. In fact, he was a young rookie detective on that case, and didn't hide the fact that he thought Valli should have been found guilty of the murder of Samuel Davis, the man who tried to attack and rape her. He insinuated at the trial that she should have called the police while she held the gun on Sam, instead of taking the law into her own hands and shooting him. However, she testified Sam came at her even after she warned him to stop, and the jury had more than enough sympathy for a young, defenseless woman who was about to be raped by a drunken slob, than the wet behind the ears rookie detective trying to be a big shot in court. But now he had another chance to bring her down and he wasn't about to give up so easy this time!

"That case has absolutely NOTHING to do with the present, and in case you forgot, Detective Reuben, I was acquitted of that charge," Valli curtly shot back.

"Yes, I remember Ms. Heart, but it's been my experience that once a killer – always a killer, and history has a way of repeating itself. We'll see just how much sympathy the jury has for a SECOND-time offender!"

A tap on the interrogation room window came just in time to keep Valli from losing her religion with Detective Reuben. Thankfully, he was being summoned outside to confer with Captain Brown.

With Detective Reuben finally out of the room, Valli quietly cried out to God to help clear her name AND find Jack's real killer. She also prayed it wasn't Seth, even though in her heart she knew it was. It HAD to be him. He was the ONLY one with enough motive to want Jack dead - besides her, and the guts and gun to do it! She didn't want to believe the man she loved could be a cold-blooded killer, but even if he was, it didn't matter. She loved Seth and vowed to stand by him – no matter what. A few moments later, Detective Reuben and Captain Brown both stepped back into the room.

"Ms. Heart, seems you were right. Preliminary ballistics report just confirmed that your gun was NOT the one used in the shooting. You are free to go, but please don't leave town, as we may need to question you further as the investigation continues. We apologize for any inconvenience you have been caused."

Valli looked over at Detective Reuben and smirked. He glared back, and she knew she hadn't heard the last of him yet. He wasn't going to give up that easy! Not this time!

"Thank you, Captain Brown. I'm not going anywhere. I'll be more than happy to answer any further questions you may have," she sweetly replied. She turned to leave, then stopped.

"Oh, yeah - may I have my gun back, please?"

"I'm afraid not, Ms. Heart. It's still considered a part of the crime scene and can't be returned just yet - at least not until the case has been solved. I trust you won't be needing a gun for anything soon, I hope?"

She glanced over once more at Detective Reuben, who was standing there with his arms crossed tightly across his chest, wearing the same smirky grin she had cast him earlier. She couldn't stand the sight of him and turned back to answer the Captain in the sweetest voice she could muster.

"No, Captain, of course not. But it was given to me by my father, and it has great sentimental value. I would like it back as soon as possible, if that's no problem."

"Not at all. We'll make sure it's returned to you, Ms. Heart – just as soon as we find Jack Conova's killer," the Captain assured her. "Now, I'm sure you have things to do - shall I escort you out?"

As Valli was being escorted to the main lobby by Captain Brown and Detective Reuben, Seth and his attorney came rushing through the front double doors of the police station.

"Valli – what's going on? Are you alright? Where are they taking you?!"

"It's alright, Seth – I'm fine." She pointed to the Captain. "This is Captain Brown and Detective Reuben. They just wanted to ask me some questions about Jack, that's all."

Seth stuck out his hand to Captain Brown. "Hello Captain, I'm Seth Spencer. This is my attorney, Chad Collins. Sorry for interrupting like this, but I can assure you Valli hasn't done anything wrong."

"Relax Mr. Spencer – we just needed to ask Ms. Heart some questions, since she and Mr. Conova were so "close". She has been cleared of any wrong doing - for the time being. We were just escorting her out. How, if I may I ask, sir, are YOU involved in this matter?"

Seth subtly glanced over at Valli. Her shifting blue eyes warned him to be careful with his words – just as he had warned her earlier.

"Uh, well, I'm just a business acquaintance of Jack and Ms. Heart's. We were working on a business deal together, and I was supposed to meet with them tonight for dinner, that's all. Then I got Ms. Heart's call a little while ago that someone had murdered Jack. I immediately called Chad, and we rushed right over to her office to see if we could be of any help."

His casual explanation didn't sit well with Detective Reuben, who was more than eager to interrogate any possible suspect - especially one connected to Valli Heart! He immediately jumped on Seth.

"Oh, is that right? Well, Mr. Spencer, we may need to question you as well, I mean if it's no inconvenience! Would you mind answering a few questions since you're already here?" Seth looked over at his lawyer who nodded his head okay.

"Of course, Detective, as long as my attorney can come with us."

"By all means. If you think you might need him." Detective Reuben didn't like the idea, but willingly obliged, just to get the interview.

"Oh, it's not that, exactly – I just want to make sure my rights are protected in every way, Detective. Sometimes, a person's words can be taken "out of context", if you know what I mean?" Detective Reuben easily read through the lines of that comment like a lace curtain, and suspected Seth Spencer already knew more than he was saying.

"Besides, I am willing to do anything I can do to help protect Ms. Heart's interest, and mine." He once again glanced over at Valli and casually winked, which didn't go unnoticed by Detective Reuben.

"Thank you, Seth – that's very kind. I'll call you later about Jack's arrangements."

Seth and Chad followed Captain Brown and Detective Reuben back to the interrogation room. He secretly wished he could have had more time to talk to Valli before being questioned but felt better that Chad was there to protect his rights and prevent him from giving away any "unnecessary" information.

Once behind closed doors, Detective Reuben bared down on Seth to try and uncover the REAL connection between him and Valli, knowing his first interrogation could be his last.

"So, Mr. Spencer, do you always take your lawyer around with you everywhere you go?" Chad immediately went for a rebuttal. "You don't have to answer that, Seth."

"It's okay Chad. I have nothing to hide." He smiled warmly back at Detective Reuben, not about to let some rude-mouthed detective trick him into saying things that could be used against him. Besides, he DIDN'T have anything to hide where Jack's murder was concerned.

"Detective, Mr. Collins came here for me AND Ms. Heart."

"And just why did you think Ms. Heart would need a lawyer?" Detective Reuben shot back. Seth gritted his teeth but managed to maintain his composure.

"Oh, you know – in case some tough-talking, hard-nosed Detective tried to bully her into saying things that aren't true." Detective Reuben glared back but didn't say a word.

Fearing Detective Reuben was coming down too hard too soon, Captain Brown broke in. "So, how well DID you know Mr. Conova, Mr. Spencer?"

"Like I just told you, he was a business associate. We were doing business together and I was about to make a sizable investment in Heart Winery. We were all getting together this evening for a celebratory dinner."

"And how long had you known Mr. Conova prior to that?" Captain Brown continued.

"Not long – maybe a few months. We met at a party one night on my yacht." His answers were short and curt, just like Chad had instructed him to answer on the way over to the station. He already figured once the cops knew about his business relationship with Heart Winery, he would be interrogated.

Detective Reuben once again took the lead. "And what about Ms. Heart. How well did you know HER?"

Seth nervously shuffled his feet under the table. His forehead beaded with warm sweat from the hot fluorescent lights above, and the poignant line of questioning from both the Captain and Detective.

"I met Ms. Heart earlier this morning at a marketing presentation she and Jack gave at Heart Winery." The lie spilled effortlessly from his lips.

"So, you JUST met her this morning, yet when she called to tell you about Conova, you felt obligated to rush right down to her office WITH your attorney along, in case SHE needed one? That's mighty considerate of you, sir." Detective Reuben's sarcasm was quickly wearing Seth down.

"I'll ask you again, Mr. Spencer – why did you think Ms. Heart might need an attorney, and why did you feel like it was YOUR responsibility to bring her one?"

Detective Reuben kept pressuring, remembering the friendly wink he saw Seth give Valli in the lobby earlier. His detective gut intuition told him there was something MORE going on between Valli and Seth, but he had nothing to prove it. Not yet, anyway. Likewise, Seth sensed Detective Reuben was highly suspicious, and turned to Chad for a rebuttal to the Detective's highly insinuating line of questioning. Chad immediately came to his rescue.

"Detective Reuben, unless you have some tangible evidence as to why you suspect my client of committing a crime, I suggest you back off with your insulting insinuations."

"Oh, I'm not insinuating anything, Counselor. I'm just trying to figure out the relationship between everyone if you have no objections. And may I remind you that your client is not under arrest, nor has he been brought in involuntarily, but of his own free will. I would appreciate it if you would allow HIM to answer the questions in his own words!"

Seeing that Detective Reuben was determined to find answers, and needing to get him off the warpath, Seth tried to diffuse the intense interrogation with a reasonable explanation.

"Look, Detective, I am a very wealthy man, and my attorney and I meet on a regular basis to discuss various legal matters pertaining to my interests and lifestyle. So naturally when I saw Ms. Heart being taken into custody and having just conducted a major business affair with her company, I wanted to protect my interests, as well as HERS. Most people do not always have a lawyer at their disposal, so I took it upon myself to make mine available to her. It's as simple as that, so please do not try to make anything more of it."

Irritated that he wasn't getting anywhere with Spencer – especially with his attorney in the room, Detective Reuben decided to dig deeper to see how much Seth knew about Valli Heart.

"Mr. Spencer, were you aware that Ms. Heart was arrested for murder twenty-five years ago?" Seth widened his eyes, attempting to look surprised, even though Valli had already confided in him about that formidable night.

"No, I wasn't aware of that. Who did she kill?"

"Samuel Davis, her mother's lover. Shot him point blank in the chest – the very same way Jack Conova was murdered." Attorney Collins promptly interrupted.

"But as I recall Detective, Mr. Davis was trying to rape and possibly kill Ms. Heart. The jury ruled she was acting in self-defense, and she was acquitted of those charges."

Both Chad and Seth crossed their arms and smugly glared at Detective Reuben. Seeing he wasn't going to get anywhere with Seth's attorney in the room, Detective Reuben decided to postpone further questioning until he could get him alone AND do a little more digging into his REAL relationship with Valli Heart.

"Okay, Mr. Spencer, I think that's all I need from you today. You've been a great deal of help!" he smirked in his usual sarcastic tone. "I'll call you if I need to talk with you further." Seth quietly breathed a sigh of relief to himself.

"Certainly, Detective, glad to have been some help. Call me anytime! C'mon Chad, let's get out of here!" Seth said, bolting from his chair, and out the door.

"You know he's not going to give up THAT easy!" Chad told Seth on the way out of the station.

"Yeah, I know – but at least I got him off my back for now! Right now, though, I've got to get to Valli, and find out what SHE told them.

He's fishing for something and I've got to make sure Valli didn't give him any BAIT!"

Chapter 10

"Wait a minute – you think I was the one that killed Jack?" Seth vehemently questioned Valli later that evening at his yacht. He couldn't believe Valli was accusing HIM of MURDER!

"That's rich coming from you, Valli. You know, YOU had more motive to kill him than I did!" he sternly reminded her. Valli was taken aback by his defensive behavior. She was so SURE he was the one who murdered Jack!

"You mean it WASN'T you?!" she exclaimed in stark surprise. She struggled to find the right words to defend such a strong accusation.

"I... I just assumed Jack called you after I talked with him and told you of our plans to meet. I figured he must have said something to set you off and you snapped!" She was SO sure she had it all figured out, and Seth's shocked and defensive reaction was NOT what she was expecting.

"Yeah, about that - just why DID you call him, Valli? What did you possibly hope to gain by meeting with him? You know that WASN'T part of our plan, sweetheart!" He tried to be patient with her, but her careless accusations insulted and hurt him. Once again, she hopelessly tried to explain her foolish reasoning for calling Jack.

"I was hoping to talk some sense into him – you know – try to get him to come over to OUR side so we could still go through with our plans. You know what they say – "keep your friends close, and your enemies closer!" She let out a lighthearted laugh, hoping to diffuse his anger. But Seth was NOT amused.

"Why would he go along with that, Valli – he was holding all the cards!"

"Yeah, I know. He reminded me of that when we spoke on the phone. I just thought I could reason with him and keep him from running his mouth about our affair." She grabbed Seth's hands and pleaded with him to understand. "I just HAD to do SOMETHING Seth! If he blabs about that affair we had, it could ruin us BOTH!"

It was the first time Valli had the guts to call it what it was– an affair. Only Jack wasn't the one fooling around – SHE was.

Jack had only been married a couple of months to Morgan Oliver, a pretty, petite brunette who used to work in the accounting department at Heart Winery. It was a whirlwind romance, and it was only after Jack and Morgan went to Vegas and got married, that Valli realized her true feelings for him. She had tried so hard to fight it, knowing it was wrong to lust after a married man, but the "flesh was weak", and she secretly began fantasizing about her and Jack. Her mind – and body – became filled with lust, and she started flirting with him every chance she got. Jack tried to discourage her, but the more he pushed her away, the more of a challenge he became, and her heart pined after him even more. She even went so far as to fire Morgan for "incompetency" in her job, secretly hoping to clear the path of anyone standing in her way. Naturally, Jack was furious with her for letting Morgan go, but knew he couldn't ruffle any feathers if he was to one day gain control of Heart Winery. So, he let it go, and convinced Morgan to do the same, promising her that one day he'd get even with Valli.

With Morgan finally out of the picture, Valli couldn't restrain her feelings any longer, and devised a calculating scheme to seduce Jack, hopefully making him forget all about her, and convincing him that SHE was the only woman for him!

One night, she lured him to her office to get his help with a "last minute" marketing project. At first, he refused to come, but Valli insisted his vast wine knowledge and input was vital, stroking his conceited ego. Jack Conova never COULD refuse shameless praise.

However, when he got to her office, the lights were dim and Valli was waiting for him in the shadows wearing nothing but a long, slinky, bust-revealing black lace negligee and cradling a bottle of fine red wine. With soulful jazz playing in the background, and the overpowering essence of her jasmine perfume wafting through the room, Jack Conova quickly became a helpless victim in her sinful web of lust and deceit.

Her catty moves were deliberate and scheming. She took Jack into her embrace and began teasing him with her hot, fiery tongue. Her moist, hungry lips caressed his, and then slid slowly and sensuously down every delicious inch of his body. His back arched with delight as her wandering tongue continued its journey downward. When her fingers grasped the button to his trousers, his breath quickened, and his body quivered in naughty anticipation. Valli became more and more aggressive as she was sure she was about to experience heaven on earth right there in her office.

She pulled Jack to the floor and threw herself on top of him. No man had EVER turned her on like Jack Conova, and she couldn't wait to have him all to herself. She begged him to touch her, forcing his hands to caress her swollen breasts through her thin gown. She was so aroused – like a caged animal - and ready for Jack to release her into his hungry embrace. How she had wanted him for so long!

But Jack shut her down. Shut. Down. Hard.

A sudden attack of guilt overcame him, and he coldly pushed her away, almost slamming her into the wall behind her. His one minute of ecstasy had turned to anger and rage.

"Sorry, Valli, but this isn't going to happen. I'm married – happily married – and you're NOT going to ruin that for me!" he angrily announced.

She remembered his sharp words cutting through her heart like a cold, icy dagger. She remembered the way he glared at her – in shame and disgust – and how he then lectured her on her sordid behavior.

"You should be ashamed of yourself, Valli! How could you come onto me, knowing I just got married? What would your father say if he knew you were trying to seduce a married man? Don't you have any decency at all?" His words spanked her like an ill-behaved child as she lay there half naked, shunned, and embarrassed by the man she so desperately wanted to love her.

About that time, Morgan busted in on them. She had tried to reach Jack earlier and when she couldn't get him, tracked him down to Valli's office. And even though Jack tried to explain what was NOT going on, Morgan was livid at the disgusting sight she witnessed, and refused to believe him. The next day she shot straight to a lawyer, and had the marriage annulled. She eventually met another man, and moved out of the country, leaving a scorned husband behind.

Jack was heartbroken – and furious with Valli for destroying his marriage. He vehemently threatened to expose her scandalous behavior to the local newspaper, which would have surely drug the Heart name through the mud and put a bloody dagger in the "heart" of Heart Winery.

Valli begged and pleaded with him to forgive her, and even promised she would talk to Morgan and try to explain things. Finally, after considering the future damage he could do to HIMSELF if he went public with such a scandalous event, he decided it was best if he said nothing and worked toward a "greater end". He ultimately forgave Valli but promised her she would be forever in "his debt".

Shunned, embarrassed and ashamed, Valli vowed never again to let Jack Conova -or any other man, ride roughshod over her heart. And that was when she metaphorically sealed her "heart in a bottle", corked with an unbreakable seal.

That was, until Seth Spencer came along.

With just one impetuous wink, Valli knew it was finally safe to release the enslaved heart she had protected all those years and take another chance on love. And even though that sordid night with Jack seem to overshadow everything else in her life, she was secretly glad he was finally dead – carrying his vicious threats to the grave with him!

Realizing how wrong she was about Seth, she buried her face in her hands, and softly cried. Seth felt a deep pang of remorse for chastising her so harshly. He pulled her into his strong arms and held her tight, hidden safely in his sheltered embrace. Finally, her soul was free to release the imprisoned tears from all those years of pent up guilt, pain, and anguish of the reckless actions of her past, as well as her current conundrum with Jack. Trapped in yet another tangled web of sin and deception, her future hopes of happiness and peace of mind hung delicately in the balance of truth and lies. She desperately needed validation that she was still a decent human being but was sure God must have already given up her.

Chapter 11

"They're hiding something - BOTH of them!" Detective Reuben told Captain Brown after the brief interrogation of Seth Spencer. The Captain agreed.

"Yeah, I think so too. But they're obviously not going to tell us, so we're going to have to find someone else who WILL talk." He paced the floor for a few moments in concentrated thought. His careful steps ushered in an overlooked detail. He stopped and snapped his bony fingers excitedly at Detective Reuben.

"Wait a minute - wasn't Jack Conova married at one time? Seems like I remember seeing his wedding announcement in the newspaper!"

"Yeah – it seems like I DO recall seeing that, too!" The foggy memory excited Detective Reuben. "He married some girl that used to work at Heart Winery, didn't he? But I don't think it lasted. I heard she had an affair or something and ran off to the Bahamas with some rich dude. Why? You think she might know something?"

"I don't know. It could be a dead end, but it's a lead we need to follow. See if you can find this girl. Maybe she can give us some "inside information" on Jack Conova and Valli Heart. If she was married to Conova - even briefly - and she worked for Heart Winery, she's got a story. Anything she can tell us may be helpful!"

"You got it, Captain. I'll see if I can track her down." Detective Reuben was like a dog with a new bone, ready to chow down on any raw meat!

"There's something else, too. We've got a dead body, and no one to step forward to claim it. Did this guy have any family around?"

"I already checked into that, Captain. Seems he's an only child, and both his parents were in bad health. They died some years ago, while he was still in college. I'll see if I can locate any distance relatives, along with his former wife, too."

"Good deal. You let me know as soon as you find out anything about Conova's ex. We need a good solid lead soon — before we have a cold body AND a cold case!"

Detective Reuben immediately went back to his office and started trying to track down the former Mrs. Conova, Morgan Oliver. After hours of searching online leads he found a recent photo of her on a popular social media site. Further research tracked her last whereabouts to the Bahamas, just as he'd heard, but more recent records showed she had left there, and was working as a waitress at the Interstate 95 Grill, a seedy truck stop diner just outside Crescent Beach. It might be a long shot, he thought, but a good detective NEVER leaves any stone unturned — even if it takes him to a cockroach infested truck stop!

On a detective's whim, he jumped in his car and thirty minutes later was sitting at the counter bar in the I-95 Grill, scouting faces for Morgan Oliver. His whim was right. There she was, sitting at a corner booth, sipping a cup of coffee. She was wearing a white waitress uniform indicating she did indeed work there. It was obvious she was on a break, so he knew he needed to act quickly before she got busy with customers. He casually walked over to her booth and sat down in the empty seat across from her. She looked over at him but didn't say a word.

"You Morgan Oliver?" His tone was firm, but non-threatening.

"Who wants to know?" she coldly replied, staring aimlessly out the window beside her.

Detective Reuben reached in his coat pocket and quickly flashed his credentials.

"Detective Joe Reuben, Crescent Beach PD. Do you know a man by the name of Jack Conova?" Morgan didn't immediately answer, wondering whether she should acknowledge she knew Jack or not. Curiosity finally got the better of her.

"Yeah, I KNEW him – used to be married to the two-timing cheating jerk!" she finally replied.

Detective Reuben looked at her curiously. The story he had heard was that SHE was the one caught cheating and ran off with her lover. Maybe there was MORE to the story. He wanted to press for details but didn't want to scare her off.

"Ms. Oliver, were you aware that your ex-husband was found shot to death Friday night?" Morgan looked surprised but didn't appear to deeply moved or shocked by the news. Her response was suspiciously disconcerting to Detective Reuben.

"No. I wasn't. We don't get that much exciting news way out here," She took another sip of coffee and checked her watch.

"That's it? Your ex-husband was just murdered and that's all you've got to say?" Aren't you the least bit curious?"

"What do you want me to say, Detective? I told you - he cheated on me. I'm not too surprised to hear someone done him in. He probably got caught cheating on another poor fool, and her old man took him out. If so, he got what was coming to him. I really could care LESS!" The fire darting from her eyes enunciated her indifference. It was obvious her concern for Jack Conova was anything BUT touching, which to Detective Reuben made her seem even MORE of a suspect!

"When's the last time you saw or spoke to your former husband?" She sighed in disgust as Detective Reuben continued his barrage of typical police questions.

"About a year ago – when I told him to take his trashy girlfriend and get the hell out of my life!" she snarled back. A crimson pink glow spread quickly across her fair ivory complexion as Detective Reuben pressed harder for more details.

"So, HE was having an affair?"

"Yes – with that snarky bitch, Valli Heart. I caught them half naked in her office one night. Both all over each other - his pants unzipped, her boobs hanging all out a sleazy negligee, having cheap thrills over a bottle of their cheap wine! They were disgusting! Of COURSE, they were having an affair; it sure didn't look like a "business meeting", if that's what you mean!"

"Did you confront him about what was going on?"

"Oh yeah – and of course, he tried to deny anything was going on, the lying jerk! But I'm not blind – I could see right through them like a lace curtain. That's when I gave him the boot and took off. You know what they say about "three's a crowd!""

"How well did you know Valli Heart, Ms. Oliver?" Detective Reuben continued.

"Well, apparently, not well enough, Detective! I worked at Heart Winery for a while, but she fired me saying I wasn't doing a good job! Then she even had the nerve to come to me after she tried to seduce my husband, and tried to say I had it all wrong, and that I should forgive Jack and go back to him. Ha! She must have thought I was a fool! As far as I'm concerned, he can burn in hell, and it's too bad whoever killed him, didn't get HER, too!" The words spewed from her lips like bile, and she held nothing back except the bitter tears of a scorned brokenhearted woman.

"Your concern is very touching," Detective Reuben scoffed.

Morgan rolled her eyes, checked her watch again, and stood up to leave, quickly tiring of his presence - and his interrogation.

"Detective, I've really got to get back to work. Why don't you just cut to the chase and tell me why you're REALLY here. What exactly do you want to know?"

"Okay, fair enough, Ms. Oliver. Where were you on Friday night?"

"Right here – where I ALWAYS am on Friday night – dishing out greasy burgers to even greasier truck drivers! You can check it out with Big Ed in the back – he's the owner. I haven't missed a Friday night working in over three months. Anything else you want to know?" she huffed, crossing her arms in front of her.

"Yeah, just one more thing. Do you own a gun, Ms. Oliver?"

"Yes, of course I do. You don't think I'd work in a seedy joint like this and not carry a gun, do you?"

"What kind of gun is it?"

"A .38 revolver – hot pink. And yes, I've got a permit for it, too – just check the records. And NO, I didn't kill Jack, if that's your next question, although I can't say the thought didn't cross my mind that night I found him with Valli! Uh, would you like to sniff the barrel of my gun?"

"No, that won't be necessary, but I may need to talk with you again when you have more time, if that's possible."

"Yeah, whatever. But right now, I've got to get back to work. Nice chatting with you, Detective – I hope you find the trigger man who killed Jack - I'd like to personally thank him!"

With all that raging hostility coming from Morgan Oliver, Detective Reuben was even MORE convinced that she, more than anyone, had a strong motive for wanting Jack Conova dead. But if she WAS working the night he was killed, her M.O. was lacking in opportunity. Not to mention she carried a .38 revolver, and ballistics proved Jack was killed with a 9mm handgun. Not that she couldn't have used another gun – after all, it would be more than stupid to use her own gun to murder someone, not to mention offer to let the police check it out.

No, something didn't add up right with her facts. They were too solid, and that was usually the first sign of a high-profile suspect. As much as he disliked Morgan Oliver, he knew their paths would have to cross again. With nothing more to gain from his visit with her, he stepped to the back to find her boss, Big Ed, to verify her whereabouts on the night of the murder. He found him in the back office, snoring loudly from a leather desk chair, his feet propped up on a nearby desk. Detective Reuben wrapped loudly on the door casing.

"You Big Ed?"

The man in the chair snorted a couple of times, swung around in the chair, and squinted up at the Detective. His scraggly gray beard and disheveled salt and pepper hair gave him the appearance of an old elderly man, though he couldn't have been much older than fifty or fifty-five. When he stood up, he looked to be at least six feet ten, carrying a twelve-month pregnant belly on his lanky five feet of giraffe-tall legs. He picked up a half-smoked cigarette from an ashtray sitting on the desk, relit it, and inhaled a few ample tokes before answering.

"Yeah, I'm Big Ed. Who are YOU?"

His voice was as scruffy as his hair, and as he talked, he blew large plumes of cigarette smoke directly in Detective Reuben's direction. A strong scent of stale whiskey accompanied the smoke streams, and Detective Reuben politely took three steps backwards so as not to get high.

"Detective Reuben – Crescent Beach P.D. I need to ask you a few questions about one of your employees – Morgan Oliver."

Big Ed raised a furry eyebrow "Oh yeah, like what? She ain't done nothing!"

"I didn't say she had, sir. I just want to know where she was Friday night, and she said you would verify her whereabouts." Big Ed took one last puff of his cigarette, dropped the butt to the floor, and stomped it out with his size twelve work boots.

"Okay, yeah, right. Well, she was here, of course – working. She ALWAYS works Friday nights – good tips, you know!"

Detective Reuben studied Big Ed's face for a flicker of truth but felt like the REAL truth was well hidden in the foggy smoke fumes that still permeated the room.

"Yeah, right. You don't mind if I take a peek at the work schedule for that night - just to see for myself, do you?"

"We don't have no schedule here. Never have. The girls just work it out between themselves."

"No schedule? You mean they don't have regularly scheduled hours to work? How do you know how many hours to pay them for then?" Big Ed grinned back at Detective Reuben, knowing he was fishing for incriminating information.

"They work on commission only – and tips. They like it that way. They don't keep no schedule – just work it out between themselves. And Morgan Oliver was here last Friday night – just like I said. Anything else you want to know, Detective?"

Big Ed just stood there and stared a blank hole through Detective Reuben. It was obvious he was covering for Morgan, and even worse, there was no paper trail to prove or disprove anything he was saying. Detective Reuben wanted to push Big Ed for more details but decided to back off and let him sweat a little. In his experience, that's when criminals were MORE likely to do the MOST talking. He felt sure he'd get another chance to chat with Big Ed in the near future.

"No, there's nothing else. Thank you for your time. I'll let you get back to your work – or whatever else it was you were doing," Detective Reuben answered with a sarcastic grin. Big Ed shrugged his shoulders, returned to his chair, and promptly resumed his beforehand interrupted nap.

Satisfied he had all the information he could get for the time being, Detective Reuben headed back to the station. On the way back, he called Captain Brown to report his findings about Morgan Oliver.

"Hey Captain – guess what - I found Morgan Oliver!"

"Oh really? She still in the Bahamas sipping fruity wine coolers with her rich lover?" the Captain joked.

"Not exactly. As a matter of fact, she's BACK in Crescent Beach, working at the I-95 truck stop just outside town!"

"Oh yeah? You go see her?"

"Yeah – I paid her a little visit. Looks like your hunch was right – she DID have quite a story to tell me! It seems SHE'S the one that got jilted – not the other way around. And by none other than our dead man - Jack Conova!"

"Really? How interesting!" Captain Brown's hunch was right – as usual.

"Wait till you hear the rest of it!" Detective Reuben was about to bust a gasket to dump all the dirt on Jack and Valli's sordid affair.

"He was having an affair with none other than our infamous wine lady, Valli Heart! She's the ONE that caused Morgan Oliver to dump Jack Conova!"

"Oh really, now?! Now we've got something to work! And Valli Heart has some explaining to do! Good work, Detective, damn good work!"

Detective Reuben smiled smugly at himself in the rear-view mirror of his patrol car. Finally, after all those years, he could put Valli Heart in her place – and he hoped that place would be a 6 x 8 jail cell in the state prison!

Chapter 12

It was a gorgeous, sunburst-filled morning, and Valli headed to her office early to retrieve some files she needed for work. Since her office was now a crime scene, Captain Brown suggested she find somewhere else to do her work until the murder investigation was over. However, when she arrived at her office, Detective Reuben and the CSI unit were still there finishing up the crime scene investigation, and she wasn't allowed in.

No sense wasting a perfectly gorgeous day! She went back to her car, put on the extra pair of tennis shoes she always kept in the trunk, and took off down the deserted beach to clear her head of the past few day's harrowing events.

Pacing nomadically in the sea-washed tracks of beach wanderers before her, she secretly wished Seth was walking alongside her down the sun-glistened shore. It seemed like days since she'd talked to him, and she longed to feel his strong, comforting arms around her anxiety-ridden body. But she knew Detective Reuben was probably watching their every move, and they couldn't risk being seen together until Jack's killer was found.

Which led her to wonder just WHO that really was? She was sure Seth had done it, but as it turned out, he had an airtight alibi for the time Jack was killed. Apparently, he was on a Skype call with another business associate, and as with all his important calls, was recorded. Captain Brown had viewed the call and verified Seth was indeed on the call for nearly thirty minutes during the suspected time Jack was murdered. He only left his office after Valli called him to tell him about Jack. Detective Reuben had also checked out his guns and his two prized 9mm handguns were securely locked in the gun safe with no evidence of either being recently fired. If he HAD killed Jack, he used a different gun, then disposed of the murder weapon quickly afterwards.

No! She quickly dismissed the absurd thought and chided herself for still believing Seth could even commit such a crime! Besides having an upstanding business reputation, and a successful yacht club, not to mention a small fortune to lose, Seth was a good Christian man, with a strong position on criminal activity - especially cold-blooded murder. He simply was NOT a murderer!

And neither was Valli, for that matter. In fact, it took her many years just to forgive herself for killing Samuel Davis – the man who nearly raped and killed HER. And yes, even though she had a fleeting desire at times to kill Jack, it was a nonsensical fantasy, at best. She knew she could never again bring herself to pull the trigger of a gun to take a man's life – no matter how much she hated him.

Still one thing deeply troubled her. How could she claim to be a "good Christian" all these years when she was secretly having a torrid love affair with Seth, AND plotting with him to get rid of Jack? No, it wasn't murder, but a sin is a sin, and in God's eyes, she must be as guilty as the one who killed Jack. Oh boy, was her conscience ever working overtime! As much as she tried to rationalize it, and defend her actions, she knew in her heart that what she and Seth were doing wasn't right, even though what Jack had been trying to do was just as wrong.

Tired of walking, she plopped down on the grassy knoll of the sand dunes and looked out over the vast blue ocean before her. Such beauty and strength emanated from the massive sea, and as always, she was in such awe of God's magnificent power! How could anyone even deny His existence when looking at such a beautiful and glorious sight? For the first time in days, she allowed herself the luxury of shutting out everything that had happened in her life, and just focusing on the pure goodness and transcendent power of God.

She shut her eyes tight and let the rhythmic sound of the undulating waves gradually fill up each one of her senses. Like a mermaid, she became as one with the ocean and felt an overwhelming sense of peace and calmness flow freely through every inch of her mind and body. She opened wide her dusty lungs, and breathed in the fresh, pure ocean air until it filled every crook and crevice of her nostrils. She threw back her head and lifted her naked face to soak up the healthy nutrients from the healing rays of the sun.

In a childhood flashback, she remembered how her father told her that the grapes closest to the sun were the sweetest and the happiest because they were so close to God. She knew now just what he meant. She had never felt as close to God as she did at that very minute. And ashamed. With her eyes still closed, and warm tears streaming down her sun-drenched face, she prayed a meager prayer of repentance and restoration.

"Dear God, please forgive me. I have been so selfish about my own wants that I have sinned against You in so many ways. I know you are disappointed in the way I've secretly lived in sin and plotted against Jack. You have brought me through so many trials in my life, and blessed me so much, and yet here I am scheming and plotting with another man to get rid of Jack. I am so ashamed of what I've let myself become, and I earnestly ask your forgiveness."

More tears fell as she released the weighty shame and guilt that had anchored her heart and soul for over twenty-five years. So ashamed was she that she didn't even know if God was listening - or if He was, would accept her pitiful prayer. She continued anyway.

"Lord, I also ask you to help me be a better woman than the woman you've seen these past few years. Please give me the strength to rise above the past, take responsibility for what I've done in the present, and make better decisions in the future. I promise I will try harder to be the woman you want me to be, living only for YOUR will, not my own. Please accept my humble prayer in Jesus name, Amen."

For the next hour, Valli sat motionless on the sand, and took it all in; the hungry seagulls scurrying the seashore looking for food, the giddy lovers walking hand in hand, and the seasoned fisherman casting their lines from the pier in the distance. And she talked to God. Not in the audible sense, but with her heart. Really talked. She realized that He was as close to her as the sand was to the sea, and that she could call on Him anytime she needed help, advice, or just someone to talk to. You might say she finally found the God she always wanted and needed, and He had been right there on the beach her whole life!

Finally feeling at peace again with the world, she lifted herself from the sand and continued her walk back to her car. For the first time in a long time, her mind was not a mottled mess of thoughts. It was clear and alert, and she knew without a doubt what her next step should be. She had to come clean about Seth. She had a strong conviction to go to Captain Brown and tell him everything. She WANTED to tell him everything. How she and Seth had been secretly seeing each other for so long, and how they had been plotting against Jack to get the secret recipe for Blue Merlot, and then get him out of Heart Winery. And about her and Jack - the REAL story - not the lie she made up when Jack was murdered.

She trembled when she thought about how she was about to shoot a deadly arrow in Seth's heart, as well as her father's company. She was at risk of losing it all, but she had promised God she would do the right thing, and she knew she couldn't go back on that promise. Her moral conviction was stronger than ever before, and she was determined to show God she had changed. But would Seth feel the same way? There was only one way to find out.

She got in her car, grabbed her cell phone from her purse and while she still had her nerve up, dialed Seth's number. She nervously bit her sun-parched lips while she waited for him to answer.

"Valli, sweetheart, how are you? Is everything okay? I've been so worried about you! I wanted to call, but figured the less we're seen together right now, the better." The soothing sound of his tender words almost made her change her mind, but she remembered her sacred vow to God.

"I'm fine, Seth, but no - everything is NOT okay. I've been thinking a lot about some things, and I've made a big decision I need to discuss with you, NOW!"

"What kind of decision, Valli?" He sensed an uncomfortable tone in her voice.

She hesitated. To be a marketing and advertising genius, this was one crucial presentation she was totally NOT prepared for.

"Valli, are you still there? What are you talking about, baby - what's all this about a decision you've made?"

Valli inhaled a big chunk of air and just blurted it out.

"Seth, I'm going to tell Captain Brown and Detective Reuben about us – and our plot against Jack. I can't live with this secrecy and dishonesty anymore. It's killing me, and I've got to clear my conscience. I made a promise to God and I hope you can understand."

She bit her bottom lip and waited for what she hoped would be Seth's tender approval. Instead, he ranted and raved for five solid minutes.

"NO! Valli, you CAN'T! We've come this far – you can't bail out on me now! And with Jack dead now, we've got nothing standing in our way, except finding that secret recipe to make Blue Merlot! Surely, he's got it hidden in his office somewhere, and after the cops get through snooping around, we can find it ourselves! Besides, there's absolutely NOTHING to gain by telling them about us. Our personal life is NONE of their business!" He stopped ranting just long enough to take a quick breath, then started back in.

"And just think what this kind of scandal could do to Heart Winery! Do you really want your father's good name dragged through the mud in a public display of humiliation and shame? Isn't that EXACTLY what Jack threatened to do to YOU? Why would you want to put yourself – and ME - in that exact same position? What can you possibly hope to gain from exposing us like this, Valli? What on earth has happened to make you think this way?! Please explain, because I don't understand this at all, Valli"

Finally, there was silence on the other end of the line. Seth had stopped talking, but his words reverberated in Valli's head like a steel drum. When the pounding subsided, she tried to make him understand.

"Seth, I know you probably won't understand this darling, but I had a deep conviction from God today, and I just feel this is something I owe Him – to finally be honest and do the right thing. I know everything you're saying is true – and I realize the serious implications this could mean for everyone, but it's a risk I must take to make things right between me and God. Don't you see? I'm SO tired of all the sneaking around just to get to see you, and the lies and deception and plotting to get back at Jack. I wasn't brought up that way, Seth, and I don't want to continue down that same crooked path in the future. Yes, I've thought about my father, and he would NOT be happy with me, or proud of the way I've handled things, and he would be very disappointed in the way I've run Heart Winery. I love you Seth, but I don't like what this has done to me. There has to be some major changes made, and they have to start with ME!"

She stopped talking and held her breath to see if she had gotten through to Seth. Another lull of silence. Had he hung up?

"Seth? Are you still there?" she softly asked.

"Yes, Valli, I'm here, and I'm begging you one last time – DON'T do this! After all this is over, you and I can get married and have a respectable life together. But if you expose everything now, neither one of us will ever have the respect of this community again! Are you really willing to throw your reputation out the window just because of a little guilt trip?"

His reasoning seemed justified and plausible – as always, but for the first time since they had met, Valli found the strength from God to resist Seth's persuasive charms and stand up for what she KNEW was right.

"It's not just a little "guilt trip", Seth. It's a major moral conviction between me and God, and something I don't think you understand, or have a right to question. You don't get to decide how I should feel! And as far as you and I go, I would hope that others will think MORE highly of us because we came forward and told the truth. And if they don't, then God will send the right people in our life that can help us move forward with dignity and respect. I also know it will hurt Heart Winery, but I owe it to my father to try and keep scandal, lies and deception OUT of his company. I have faith that God will NOT let my father's legacy go down the drain over my sins. That's what it's all about in the end, Seth - trusting God to get us through this and working things out for our good - just as He promised in his Word. Now do you understand better why I have to do this?"

Again, she waited for Seth to "see the light" and respond with respect and acceptance. Instead, the phone line went dead, and she knew she had lost him – maybe for good.

Regardless, there was no turning back now. Telling Seth was the hardest part - now she had to get to Captain Brown and Detective Reuben and tell them what she knew, before she went weak again and changed her mind. She prayed for Goliath sized strength all the way over to the police station.

Chapter 13

"So, Morgan Oliver crashed in on Valli Heart and Jack Conova at her office one night?" Captain Brown asked Detective Reuben as they further discussed his meeting with Morgan Oliver.

"Yeah – she said Valli Heart was standing there wearing only a skimpy negligee and holding a bottle of wine when she busted in on them. Oh, Conova tried to deny anything was going on, but according to Oliver, his pants were unzipped, and she was half naked– you know, like they were just getting down to it!" Detective Reuben seemed to delight in all the sordid details.

"So, that gives Ms. Oliver a perfect motive for wanting Jack Conova dead. How interesting! Did you ask her about an alibi, and if she owned a gun?"

"Oh yeah – said she had a .38 Special– hot pink! Ha! Ha! Said it was registered. She even volunteered to let me "sniff the barrel"! She was WAY too obliging – if you know what I mean! As for her alibi, said she was working at the greasy diner the night of the murder."

"You check everything out?"

"Well, the gun checks out like she said - it's registered. But her work schedule details were a little sketchy."

"Sketchy – how so?"

"Well, I checked with her boss – a man she called "Big Ed", and he SAID she worked that night, but they don't punch a time clock, nor do they keep a schedule of the hours the girls work!"

"Well, how in the hell do they know how many hours to pay them if they don't keep up a time schedule?"

"He said they work on tips only, so they don't have to keep up with their hours. They just work it out between themselves, and apparently, Friday nights are one of Oliver's regular work nights. It sounded pretty fishy to me – how about you?"

"Damn fishy," the Captain agreed. "And convenient. No, I'm not buying it either. Unless this Oliver chick can get someone respectable to collaborate her whereabouts for that night, we might just have ourselves our FIRST real prime suspect in the murder of Jack Conova!"

"Yeah, but what about Valli Heart? She had a motive, too - especially now since we know SHE was the one Jack Conova was having an affair with. According to Oliver, he was LIVID with Valli for wrecking their marriage. Said Valli even came to her a few days later and tried to smooth things over with her so she wouldn't divorce Conova, but she was done with him."

"Then it seems to me like Conova would have had it in for Heart, not the other way around," Captain Brown surmised. "Why would she want to kill HIM?"

"Maybe he threatened HER, and she figured she'd kill him before he had a chance to kill her!"

"I don't know, Joe, I'll admit I think Ms. Heart is hiding something, but I don't think she's our killer."

As much as Detective Reuben wanted to have something on Valli, he knew the Captain was probably right. It did look like their prime suspect now was Morgan Oliver. Only she had an alibi – at least for the time being.

"Yes, I need to see either Captain Brown or Detective Reuben right away, please!" Valli urgently requested of the reception clerk down at police headquarters.

"I'm sorry, ma'am, but they're both in a meeting. Would you like to leave a message?"

"It's okay, Jackie, I can see her." Detective Reuben had just slipped around the corner when he saw Valli standing there.

"Detective Reuben – I need to talk to you – NOW!" Valli said, her voice cracking.

"Of course, Ms. Heart - let's go to my office."

"You may want to get Captain Brown, as well. I'm sure he'll be interested in what I have to say, too."

"Jackie, call Captain Brown and have him meet us in my office immediately!" he yelled back to the desk secretary. By the time they got to his office, Captain Brown met them at the door.

"Okay, Ms. Heart, we're both here. Tell us what's on your mind." Detective Reubens' sharp investigative instincts told him he was about to hear a confession of some sort. And by now, Valli was so full of the Holy Spirit, she was bursting at the seams to tell her story. If criminals could just get a dose of what she had, there would never be any need for lie detectors!

"It's about me and Seth Spencer." The words came spilling out easy enough but left a bad taste in her mouth - almost like regurgitating poison. She wondered if she could get the rest of them out, without getting physically ill.

"What about you and Seth Spencer?" Captain Brown asked. With Captain Brown's gentle probing, Valli found the courage to continue.

"I lied," Valli confessed. "We've known each other longer than just a few days. In fact, we've known each other for a while now. We met at a Young Singles Group meeting at my church after my father died." The thought of her father's passing still saddened her. She paused again, in tearful reverence for the only man who she ever really trusted.

"Go on, Ms. Heart – we're listening," Captain Brown coaxed.

"Well, we started seeing each other – in secret – mostly on his yacht…. and…." her crackling words trailed off, replaced with long, sorrowful sobs.

"Take your time Ms. Heart, and just tell us what's wrong," Captain Brown again urged.

Suddenly, the door busted open and in walked Seth Spencer, followed by Jackie, the front desk secretary.

"I'm SO sorry Captain, but when he found out Ms. Heart was with you, he INSISTED on seeing her and just marched himself right down to your office! I tried to stop him, but…."

"It's alright, Jackie - you're not responsible. You may go back up front." After Jackie left, Captain Brown lit in on Seth.

"What the hell is wrong with you Spencer?! I ought to have you arrested for disorderly conduct!" Captain Brown shouted.

"Excuse me for interrupting, Captain, but this is urgent. I need to see Valli - NOW!" Without waiting for a response from Captain Brown, Seth grabbed Valli by the arm and pulled her into the hallway, and quickly ushered her towards the front door.

"Valli, DON'T do this! You CAN'T do this! I need to tell you something before you ruin everything! Please, give me a chance to talk to you before you say another word to them," he whispered desperately in her ear as he hurried her out of the police station. Valli struggled to get free, but Seth's hold on her was too tight.

"Spencer – you let go of her right now or I'll have you charged with kidnapping!" Detective Reuben yelled to him from down the hall.

"It's okay, Detective – I'll come back another time!" Valli yelled back in response.

"Are you sure you want to go with him, Ms. Heart?" Captain Brown called out, hurrying down the hall with Detective Reuben.

"Yes, Captain – I'm sorry – I'll have to talk to you later!" Valli called back, as Seth hurried her outside.

"Seth, it's too late! I've ALREADY told them about us!" she confessed after they had finally made it to his car in the parking lot. Seth released his hold on her. His expression sank faster than the Titanic.

"WHAT?! You've already told them? Everything? You told them about us, and what we were planning to do to Jack? My God, Valli – what on earth have you done? You've ruined EVERYTHING! How could you?!" He leaned hard against his car and stared out into the hollow sky above. How could this woman that he loved SO much do something SO reckless?

Valli felt about two feet tall. She hated so much that Seth felt she had ruined things and was hurt herself that he still didn't understand.

"No, Seth, I didn't get to tell them EVERYTHING, but I was planning to before you came busting in. As far as I'm concerned, YOU'RE the one that's ruined everything! Why couldn't you just trust me - and God - that I was doing the RIGHT THING? Why couldn't you just give me credit just this once, Seth?" Valli was mad. Mad at Seth - and herself. Why did he have to show up and stop her from making good on her promise to God? Seth was equally as mad - but his love for Valli was stronger, and he knew he couldn't stay mad at her for long. He let out a deep breath and turned to face her, trying not to show any further anger.

"Valli, I'm sorry. Really, I am. I didn't mean to come between you and God, but there's so much you don't know. Please, come with me and let's talk, and if you still want to go talk to the Captain afterwards, I won't stop you. Please, darling…"

Valli hadn't been able to resist Seth Spencer's persuasive charms from the first day she met him, and it was no different now. She let out an exasperated sigh.

"Okay, Seth. I guess I do owe you an opportunity to have your say. Let's go talk. But I'm STILL determined to come clean with Captain Brown and Detective Reuben. I still owe God too!"

Seth opened the car door and Valli reluctantly got in. He slid in the driver's side and started the ignition. As he looked in the rear-view mirror, a dark shadow running up to the car caught his eye. It was

Detective Reuben, who was fast approaching the passenger side of the car and slapping his fist against the window.

Seth jerked the gear shift into reverse and stomped the gas pedal to the floor, nearly sending the Detective to the ground.

"Ms. Heart, where you going? You didn't finish what you were telling us!" Detective Reuben yelled out to Valli.

"Don't worry, Detective - I'll be back!" she yelled back through the cracked window as Seth kicked the super charged sports car into fifth gear and sped off like a runaway train.

Chapter 14

Safely back at his yacht, Seth settled Valli down with a tender neck massage. Her anxiety-ridden body melted beneath the soothing touch of his dexterous hands, and soon she was feeling as calm and peaceful as the ocean at low tide. Seth always seemed to have that effect on her. Just like with her father. He, too, could chase away her blues with just a warm hug or a tender kiss on her forehead. Maybe that's why she fell so deeply in love with Seth; his love replaced the love she lost when her father died, only in a different way. How could she possibly jeopardize that now by turning against him?

"Feeling better now, darling?"

"Yes, MUCH better." She let out a contented sigh, wishing he'd stroke her just a few minutes longer. Instead, he gently turned her around to face him.

"Valli, you've got to listen to me, and think this thing out. I know you have this "God-need" to come clean and all, but sometimes it's better just to leave some things unsaid - to protect people you care about."

"But Seth, that's LYING! I've always been taught to tell the truth, and whenever I try to hide something, it always just ends up worse than if I had just told the truth to start with. Don't you think we'd look LESS guilty if we just told the police what Jack was planning to do?"

"No, Valli, I don't! Look, why tell them ANYTHING? Let them figure it out! If you go blabbing everything, that bully Detective is going to stop looking for another suspect and just try and pin this on us. Remember, like he tried to do to you with Samuel Davis? He's just looking for a conviction, Valli, and if he knows we had motive and opportunity, he's going to be convinced we're guilty. We'd be playing right into his hands! Don't you see that?"

Once again, he made a complicated situation seem like a first-grade math problem. Or maybe it's just things were so jumbled in her mind, she wasn't thinking too clearly to start with.

"But they already think one of us is guilty - maybe BOTH of us. Shouldn't we at least defend ourselves?"

"We're NOT on trial, Valli - we don't NEED to defend ourselves. Look, if they REALLY thought one of us was guilty, they'd be interrogating us night and day trying to get us to confess. But I know I didn't do it, and I know YOU didn't do it, so let's just wait it out and make them find the REAL killer! It will save us BOTH a lot of headaches and legal fees if we just keep our mouths shut for now, understand? Besides, I really don't want to be involved in a long, drawn out murder trial– do YOU?"

Valli tried to reason it all out like Seth, but her head was still spinning with so many questions, and so few answers. He had given her all the RIGHT reasons NOT to talk, but she didn't feel the same conviction that hit her when she was alone with God on the beach.

"Seth, I have to go. I need some time to think about all this." She picked up her purse and headed to the door. "Please take me back to the station to get my car." Seth gently pulled her back and caressed her weary face in his hands. Once again, she was defenseless against his tender touch.

"Valli, darling, you've got to trust me on this. I respect the fact that you want to come clean and make it right between you and God, but no good can come from this. If you feel the need to confess, go down to the Catholic Church and make your confession to the priest. Or volunteer to work in a community program to make atonement for your guilt. But I'm begging you NOT to turn this into an ugly scandal that will only hurt us - and our future. Our love is strong and deserves to be protected – not battered and abused. Please don't let that happen!" Before Valli could protest, Seth pressed his warm sensuous lips to hers, and kissed her with the passion of King Solomon.

"I love you," he whispered breathlessly into her ear.

Her lips melted deeper into his until she felt swallowed up by his love. Seth once again had her under his spell, as he had done so many times before, and she was rendered helpless to sound judgment. She knew she needed to leave before her unbridled passion took over and left her totally incapable of doing what was right. Mustering all the intestinal strength she could find, she pulled away from Seth, ran to the door and quickly out of the cabin, determined not to look back. Running blindly and frantically down the pier, she just did stop before nearly colliding with Captain Brown and Detective Reuben, who were waiting at the foot of the dock.

"Well, well Ms. Heart – we had a feeling we'd find you here," Detective Reuben chided. "Perhaps now, you'd like to finish telling us about you and Seth Spencer!"

"What did you do, follow us here?" Vallie retorted angrily.

"No ma'am, we just put two and two together. You were about to confess something to us earlier when your boyfriend suddenly shows up and whisks you away. Being a detective, it wasn't too hard to figure out he was trying to keep you from telling us something he didn't want us to know!"

"Well, you're wrong," Valli snipped back. "Seth just wanted to make sure I wasn't being falsely accused of anything, and that I knew all my legal rights – that's all." Another lie she'd have to ask forgiveness for later.

"And just WHY would you need to know your rights if you hadn't committed a crime, Ms. Heart?" Detective Reuben was determined to catch her in a lie this time.

"Leave her alone! She's telling the truth!" Seth shouted as he ran up the pier to Valli's side when he saw her talking with Captain Brown and Detective Reuben. "Why aren't you two out looking for the REAL killer, instead of harassing innocent people? I should sue you BOTH for stalking!"

"Take it easy, Mr. Spencer – no one is stalking ANYBODY! We're just trying to get at the truth about what happened to Mr. Conova,"

Captain Brown calmly replied. "But if Ms. Heart doesn't have anything to hide, why do you feel the need to keep protecting her? Or maybe she's trying to protect YOU?"

"Protect ME? Why should I need protection – I haven't committed any crime!"

"Well, she's already admitted she lied about her relationship with you. It just makes us wonder what ELSE she's lied about!"

Valli once again felt God dealing with her and felt she couldn't hold her confession any longer. The secrecy, hiding and lies had to stop!

"Yes, I lied – I've lied about A LOT!" she screamed into the wide-open sky above her.

"Valli, don't!" Seth begged.

"It's too late, Seth – I can't keep on living this lie a minute longer! We HAVE to tell them what we've done!"

"Yes, please, finish telling us what you started back at the station," Captain Brown urged.

Valli took a bold step forward to face Captain Brown. Armed with God's strength, and firmly planted in her faith, she felt a spiritual boldness rise in her. This time, she would NOT let Seth or anyone else stop her from making good on her promise to God. She was ready to talk, and SOMEONE was going to LISTEN!

"Seth and I – we've been planning for months to get rid of Jack, but it's not what you think" she confessed. "All we wanted was to get his formula for the Blue Merlot wine he developed, then get him OUT of my father's company! He's been trying to blackmail me for months because his ex-wife caught us together one night and got the wrong idea. She blamed Jack, but it was really ME who tried to seduce him! But she didn't believe him, and that's when she left him and ran off to the Bahamas. I had already fired her, and was going to fire him, too, but he threatened to expose me to the public and I knew it would shame me, my father and Heart Winery. I couldn't take that risk, so I agreed to let him stay on as a junior partner. He's been looking for a way to get back at me ever since! And THAT, Captain Brown is the

TRUTH!" Valli closed her eyes momentarily, wishing the angels in Heaven would just swoop down and take her away. She was so done with all this earthly chaos!

Captain Brown exchanged a confused look with Detective Reuben. "So, you had an affair with Jack Conova. What has Seth Spencer got to do with all this?" Detective Reuben asked.

"I can answer that, Detective." Seth offered. "I was only trying to help Valli get what was rightfully hers – and get that scumbag out of her father's business! I met Valli at a church singles group and we fell in love. She confided in me and told me how Jack was trying to blackmail her into getting control of her father's company. We knew we had to find a way to get him out, but we had to get the formula for the Blue Merlot wine first. It's a proprietary blend that will substantially increase Heart Winery's position in the wine industry and give Valli a secure future. It's what her father would have wanted for her, and I wanted to help make that happen for her. We knew Jack wouldn't hand it over voluntarily – not after what happened between them, so we had to devise a plan to take it from him!"

"You mean it would secure YOUR future, too, don't you, Mr. Spencer?" Detective Reuben now turned his attention to Seth's possible motives.

"It seems to me you BOTH had a strong motive for wanting Jack Conova dead," Captain Brown added. "Are you confessing to the murder, Ms. Heart?"

"NO! Absolutely NOT – I - WE, did NOT kill Jack!" Valli insisted. "I just wanted to come clean because God has been dealing with me about all the lies and deceit Seth and I have been hiding all these months. I'm a Christian, Captain, and my first loyalty is to God – not Jack – not Seth – not even YOU! But even though I've lied about a lot of things, I'm NOT lying when I say I did NOT kill Jack Conova!"

"Yeah, yeah, they all say that," Detective Reuben taunted. "But if you ask me…."

"Yeah, hello, this is Brown." The Captain shushed Reuben as a call came through on his cell phone.

"Oh really? Are you sure? Uh-huh. No, that won't be necessary. He's right here - we'll bring him right down for questioning. Okay, yeah, thanks." Click. Captain Brown slid his phone back under his coat and stared over at Seth.

"Well, well. It looks like you're going to have to come with us, Spencer." Seth's whole face instantly twisted into a confused cartoon caricature.

"Me? Why? You've already interrogated me one time, in case you don't remember!"

"Well, this time, it's a little more justified. Just got a call from headquarters. It seems a 9 mm handgun registered to you was just found buried in the sand on the beach. And according to preliminary ballistics, it also seems to be the SAME gun used to murder Jack Conova!" Without hesitating, he firmly grabbed Seth by the arm and forced him to walk down the dock, with Detective Reuben following closely behind.

"What'd you say we take a little trip back to the station and you can tell us how your gun ended up on the beach, and how you used it to kill Jack Conova?"

Stunned and in shock, Valli could do nothing but blindly watch them go, through blurry, tear filled eyes. Confession may have been good for her soul, but it sure unleashed the demons on Seth!

"Call my lawyer, Chad, and have him meet me at the police station!" Seth called back to Valli. "His card is on the table by the bed in the yacht! And hurry!" ....

Chapter 15

Back at the police station, Detective Reuben led Seth once again to the interrogation room.

"Okay, what's this all about, Detective? Why am I a suspect in Jack Conova's death? You know I have an air-tight alibi. I was on a conference call at the time Jack was murdered. Captain Brown verified it himself. I should sue this damn place for false arrest!" Seth shouted.

"Calm down, Spencer. You'll get your day in court. But you can save us all a lot of trouble if you'll just explain how YOUR 9 mm semi-automatic handgun - the SAME one that killed Jack Conova - ended up on the beach, not far from the murder scene. A beach comber found it in the sand and turned it in to us. Ballistics confirmed it's your gun from the serial numbers. Pretty careless of you not to file those off, if you were going to use it to commit murder, don't you think?"

"Okay, look Detective. Here's the deal. I sold one of my 9 mm guns to a guy a couple about a year ago, who collects guns. So, HE'S the one you want – not ME!"

"Do you have this guy's name and contact information?"

"Well, no, it was a "private sale" and he paid me in cash. So, he hasn't had it re-registered in his name yet. What's the big deal?"

"The "big deal" Spencer, is that a gun, still registered in YOUR name, and the same kind as was used to kill Jack Conova, was found half-way buried in the sand on the beach, not forty yards from the murder scene. Not to mention, you and your girlfriend have been lying to us about your relationship AND have been secretly planning to get rid of Jack Conova. Don't you find all this sort of incriminating? What would you think if you were in MY shoes?"

Seth had to admit to himself things didn't look that good, but he wasn't about to confess to a crime he knew he didn't commit.

"Look, Detective, I know how all this must look to you, but I did NOT kill Jack Conova! I'll admit I wanted him OUT of our lives, but you've got the WRONG MAN! How can I be the murderer when I was on a Skype call at the time? You saw the video yourself! I can't be in two places at one time, now can I?"

"That doesn't necessarily mean you didn't orchestrate his murder. All we need to know is WHO you hired to do it. Do you want to come clean now, or wait till we prove it in court?"

"Don't say another word, Seth!" Finally – Chad had arrived just in time to get Detective Reuben off his back.

"We're done here, Detective. You have nothing concrete on my client, and I demand you release him at once!" Detective Reuben really didn't want to let Seth go, but he knew he needed more evidence to hold him on a solid murder charge.

"Alright, Spencer. I'm letting you go – for now. But you're still a PRIME SUSPECT. Just don't get any funny ideas about taking a vacation on one of your fancy yachts anytime soon!"

"Oh, don't worry, Detective. I'm not going anywhere. I want to be around to see YOU in court on false arrest charges! C'mon Chad, let's get out of here!" Seth turned to open the door and came face to face with Captain Brown, who had been watching the interrogation from the soundproof room next door.

"Leaving so soon, Mr. Spencer?" Captain Brown asked. Weren't you just brought in on a possible murder charge? I thought you'd be in an orange jumpsuit by now."

"Ha Ha! – very funny Captain. But you and your scumbag detective there will be sharing a cell once you're brought up on false arrest charges!"

"Yeah, yeah, right. Go on, get out of here – while you still can. Just remember what Detective Reuben told you – don't leave town. We don't want to have to track you down on one of your fancy boats!"

"C'mon, Seth, let's go," Chad urged. "Valli is waiting in the parking lot." Seth and Chad left while Detective Reuben and Captain Brown tried to figure out the missing pieces of Jack Conova's murder.

"Couldn't get a confession out of him, huh?" Captain Brown asked Detective Reuben after they had left.

"Nah, I knew it was a long shot to try and get him to confess on a phony arrest charge. He's not that dumb. We're going to have to do a little more digging to find out WHO he hired to kill Conova."

"You still think he's the killer, Joe? I mean, he does have an airtight alibi – I saw the conference video myself. His whole story checks out."

"Well, I'll admit maybe he didn't do it himself, but it was HIS gun, and him and his girlfriend DID have a motive! I figure their plan was to send a hit man up ahead of time to kill Jack, then his girlfriend would show up and act surprised and distraught to find him dead. She'd call us to report the murder, while Spencer was conveniently at his office on a Skype call. That way he would have an airtight alibi."

"Still doesn't add up, though. If a hit man took out Conova, why would he hide the gun on the beach?"

"I don't know, Captain. But it's obvious SOMEBODY was trying to get rid of it.

"Yeah, and we need to find out WHO that somebody was! Why don't you go pay the ex-Mrs. Conova another little visit? She's still a suspect, too, remember? Maybe she'll recant her story and give us some more clues to work with. Meanwhile, I've got a little visit to pay someone myself!"

"Oh yeah, like who?"

"I don't want to say just yet. You just see what else you can find out from Morgan Oliver. I'll let you know if I turn up anything else!"

"Sure thing, Captain. I'll get right on it." After Detective Reuben left, Captain Brown made a quick call.

"Yeah, Harry? Frank Brown here. You still got that surveillance camera in your penthouse office across the street from the Crescent Beach Office Towers?"

Harry Phillips owned the North Shore Hotel directly across the street from Crescent Beach Office Towers – where Valli Heart's office was. He had a plush penthouse office on the twelfth floor, complete with a surveillance camera that overlooked the entire parking lot of Crescent Beach Office Towers. If anyone was stalking Jack that night, hopefully they would show up on the surveillance footage.

"Yep, sure do – why?"

"I need to see some footage from Friday night. Mind if I come over in about an hour?"

"Not at all, Frank - I'll meet you there!"

Captain Brown knew it was a long shot, but maybe something would show up in that surveillance footage that would give him a clue as to who Jack Conova's killer was.

Chapter 16

"You! What are you doing back here again?" Morgan Oliver asked in disgust when she saw Detective Reuben sitting at the counter sipping a cup of coffee.

"Hello, Sunshine!" He figured it wouldn't hurt to try using a little "honey" to trap this scorned little bee into talking. He had a new angle too. If a hit man could do the dirty work for Seth Spencer, he could do it for Morgan Oliver, too! He had to find out more about the man she was living with in the Bahamas. Maybe together, they schemed up a plan to take out Jack Conova. It was worth a shot anyway, he figured.

"Look, Detective, I ain't got nothing else to say to you – unless you come to tell me you got Jack's murderer. In that case, I'd say "thank you." But if that ain't why you're here, then you can just leave 'cause I'm busy, as you can see."

"Chill out, Ms. Oliver – I mean Ms. Conova – or whatever you're calling yourself these days. I just stopped by for a cup of this delicious coffee, and an opportunity for us to chat again. You know, just in case you forgot to tell me something last time we talked."

"Yeah, right, Detective. You know, it doesn't take much brains to figure you guys out. You're like a nosy hound dog come snooping around looking for any kind of bone someone will throw you. So, go ahead – get it off your chest. What else do you want to know about me and Jack?"

Morgan Oliver was smarter than he gave her credit for. But seeing as how she busted in on Jack and Valli, it stood to reason she was suspicious of men. Looks like he'd have to play it straight with her. Sort of!

"Okay, doll – this time I'm the one busted. You're right – I am back looking for information. Like how your gun ended up buried in the sand on Crescent Beach, forty yards from the murder scene?"

"Nice try, but you better try again, Detective. I already told you - my gun is stored safe and sound in a private place – and NO, I'm not telling you WHERE. But I assure you it wasn't found buried in the sand on the beach!" She rolled her eyes at his laughable theory.

"Are you SURE about that, Ms. Oliver?"

"YES, I AM! Now, stop all the B.S. and quit wasting my time!"

"Okay, then, what about your boyfriend? You know, the one you were shacking up with in the Bahamas? Maybe it's HIS?" Detective Reuben was fishing for "ghost fish" - an old detective's trick.

"WHAT boyfriend? Who says I have a boyfriend, or that he has a gun?" Morgan twisted his suspicious question into a gnarly pretzel and fed it back to him.

"Well, you WERE cozy with some guy in the Bahamas not too long ago, weren't you? Maybe he's still around somewhere? And maybe you and he cooked up this whole plan to get revenge on Jack Conova for what he did to you with Valli Heart? Is that what happened, Ms. Oliver?" He tapped his fingers impatiently on the counter to hurry her reply.

"You are WAY off base Detective, and I am way too busy to play your stupid little guessing games! I think you better leave NOW, before I have you thrown out!" In true detective style, Detective Reuben kept badgering her for more details.

"What's his name, Ms. Oliver – you know, your Bahama boyfriend? You don't mind if we have a chat with him, do you?"

"What's going on here, Morgan?"

A deep voice interrupted them from the kitchen. It was Big Ed – her boss. He looked over at the counter, and recognized Detective

Reuben from an earlier conversation about Morgan Oliver's work schedule the day of the murder.

"Something we can do for you, Detective? Is there a problem with your order?"

"No, no problem here. I was just telling Ms. Oliver here how great the coffee is, and that I might have to stop by more often!"

"It's okay, Ed. There's no problem. This nice detective was sort of confused on a few things, but I think I've straightened him out. I think he's about ready to leave now, isn't that right, Detective?" Morgan promptly gave Detective Brown her "get-the-hell-out-and-don't-come-back" smile.

"Yes, I do have to be going. But, I did mean what I said about the coffee – it's very good, and I will DEFINITELY be back for another cup – SOON!" He stared intently at Morgan, making sure she knew he wasn't quite finished with her. Morgan hurried off to wait on another customer, leaving Detective Reuben alone with Big Ed.

"Tell me something, Ed – do you happen to know who Morgan Oliver went running around the Bahamas with after she split from Conova?"

"As a matter of fact, I do" Big Ed answered. "It was ME. When she got tired of sipping wine coolers over there, we decided to head back to the States and settle down. A friend of mine sold us this joint and we're planning on getting married soon. Why do you ask, Detective?"

"Oh, no reason – just curious. Oh, by the way – do you happen to own a gun, Ed?"

"Yeah, I own a gun – a 9 mm – but it's registered, and I have a permit. And before you ask, Detective, no, I did NOT kill Jack Conova – and neither did Morgan. I know what you're up to and I'm warning you to leave her alone! That two-timing sleazy playboy Conova hurt her bad and he got what he deserved! I suggest you leave us BOTH alone, and don't come back in here with anymore of your sneaky questions!"

Big Ed huffed off, leaving Detective Reuben with an empty cup of coffee, and an even emptier case against Morgan Oliver. A dead end once again.

After Detective Reuben left, Big Ed called Morgan back to the kitchen. "I don't like that nosy detective snooping around all the time. It's getting a little TOO warm around here – think maybe we should split town?"

"No, baby, we gotta stay cool or else this whole thing will blow up. Don't worry – I can take care of that detective – just don't freak out!"

"What about Jessie – how she's holding up? You don't think she's going to crack, do you? You know how nervous she can get!"

"Nah – she's cool. She knows the deal. She'll follow through with the rest of the plan if she wants her part of the "reward." Relax, baby - we ALL just gotta stay calm and play it cool until we get what we want - then we can head back to the Bahamas like we planned. But if we leave now, it will definitely throw up some red missiles!"

"Okay, babe, this is your gig; we'll do it YOUR way. We'll hang around for a little while longer. But you keep your guard up - especially around that old nosey detective! He doesn't seem like the type to give up too easy!"

Morgan shrugged as if she could care less about Detective Reuben. But deep down, she had a gnawing feeling that something was about to go VERY wrong with the cleverly schemed plan she had been working on ever since that night she caught Jack and Valli together. She was so close to getting everything she had wanted, and she couldn't afford any slip-ups now. She just hoped Jessie and Big Ed would hang with her until the end...

Back at the North Shore Hotel, Captain Brown was reviewing the surveillance footage from the Penthouse office with Harry Phillips.

"The panoramic camera does a complete 360-degree rotation, has a high-powered zoom lens, and a built-in motion detector. If anyone was going in or out of that building, we've got 'em on tape!"

"That's what I was hoping you'd say, Harry – let that footage roll, and see if we can spot a killer!"

Chapter 17

"Seth, I'm scared!" Valli buried her head deep in Seth's chest and quietly sobbed. "What if they find you guilty of Jack's murder?" Seth poured her a rounded glass of Blue Merlot wine and handed it to her.

"Here baby, drink this, and just calm down. Everything's going to be okay – I promise. Besides, I DIDN'T kill Jack! They have nothing on me and they know it. They're just grasping at straws – that's all. Captain Brown is a smart man. He knows I didn't do it and he won't stop digging till he finds the REAL killer – which is NOT ME!"

"But it was YOUR gun they found in the sand. What if they think you HIRED someone to kill Jack? You could still be implicated!"

"Don't be ridiculous, Val – I didn't hire anyone to kill Jack Conova. Why would you even think that of me? Don't you trust me more than that? Haven't I proven my love for you over and over again in the past few months? Don't you have any faith in me at all?"

"Oh, Seth, I'm so confused. I WANT to believe you, but I don't understand all this." She broke away from his embrace and stared him deadlock in the eyes.

"I love you with all my heart, and if you DID kill Jack, I promise I'll STILL love you – no matter what. But I must know – please tell me the truth – DID YOU KILL HIM?"

Seth was visibly shaken by her doubt and disbelief in him. And even though things did look bad, he never thought she would suspect him of murder! Maybe she wasn't the woman he thought she was after all. How could she claim to love him, and then call him a murderer?

"NO, Valli! Once and for all, I did NOT kill Jack Conova, and it really hurts me that you even THINK that! I'll admit I didn't really LIKE the guy, but I'm no murderer! And if you can't take my word for it, then I guess our love and trust in each other isn't as strong as I thought, and maybe I'm not the right man for you. I love you, Valli Heart, but I can't be with a woman that doesn't trust me."

Valli broke down at the thought of losing Seth – or of him leaving her. What a fool she'd been to doubt him after all the time he'd spent trying to help her regain total control of Heart Winery! She suddenly felt ashamed and foolish.

"Oh Seth, I'm sorry – I didn't mean it. I know you're not a murderer. Please, please baby don't say you're not the right man for me! There's never been a BETTER man for me – and there never will be. I believe you and I'm begging you to forgive me for doubting you!" Again, she fell into his strong arms and sobbed tears of shame in his chest.

"It's okay baby – I know this has been hard on you, and I'm sorry, too. I could NEVER love another woman like I love you, and I would rather die myself than to ever do anything to hurt you or jeopardize what we have together."

He wrapped his long arms around her trembling body even tighter, buried his face in her thick, silky blonde hair and wept his own tears of fear and doubt. He, too, feared what the future held, but he could NEVER let her know it. Seth had never been much of a praying man, but as he held Valli tight in his arms, he silently prayed that God would forgive them both for their selfish scheme and help them out of the tangled mess they were in.

Just then, like a lightning bolt from heaven, a thought occurred to him. In all the excitement and confusion of the murder investigation, no one had even mentioned looking for the secret recipe for the Blue Merlot. After all, that was the whole point of their plan – to get that recipe! And now that Jack was dead, there was nothing holding them back from taking the Blue Merlot – and Heart Winery to new heights! He pulled Valli away from his chest and snapped his fingers with delight.

"Valli – do you have a key to Jack's office at Heart Winery?"

"Why, yes – of course – I have keys to EVERYTHING at Heart Winery. Why do you ask?"

"Don't you see – we completely forgot about the secret recipe for Blue Merlot! It's got to be somewhere in Jack's office! We've got to go find it – right NOW!"

"But what about the police, Seth? Detective Reuben told me not to disturb anything in Jack's office until the investigation is over. What if he finds out we went snooping around there? Won't that look a little suspicious?"

"Why should it? Look, you're the CEO of Heart Winery, and you've STILL got a business to run, right? You have every right, not to mention a responsibility, to keep things going at Heart Winery – despite Jack's death. Surely there are documents and things in his office that you need to do that, right?"

Valli's eyes lit up like a diamond glistening in the sand on a moonlit beach. Of course! Seth was right – she DID need to get back to Heart Winery and make sure things were being run properly. After all, except for the winery supervisors, there was really no one left to take charge of Jack's position. As owner, it was her duty and responsibility to get things back on track.

"Seth, darling, you're a GENIUS! I can't believe I didn't think of that myself! My father would be so disappointed if I let things go downhill now! You're absolutely right – we've GOT to go to Jack's office, and while we're there, we might as well get that recipe!"

Seth and Valli headed over to Heart Winery as fast as they could, with the assurance that the sooner that recipe was safely in their hands, the better. However, they weren't the only ones who remembered the Blue Merlot recipe.

"Okay, doll – let's do this. You've got the key to his office, right?" Big Ed asked Morgan.

"Right here, baby!" She tossed a single silver key up in the air in front of him and winked back at him.

"Careful with that, sweetheart – that's our "key to the kingdom!""

"Don't worry, babe – I've held onto this little silver bullet since the day the copy was made. And then when Jack called me to tell me he was meeting Valli Heart at her office Friday night, and that once he "took care of her," we could be together again, I knew it was time to put our plan into motion!"

"Yeah, you played it cool, baby – letting old Jack believe you'd come back to him once he got Valli Heart out of the way. He played right into your hands! And I especially liked the part where he confided in you about that secret recipe for that Blue Merlot wine! Now all we got to do is get that recipe from his office and we can sell it to that offshore wine broker we met in the Bahamas! Then it's goodbye greasy diner, and hello five-star restaurants!" Big Ed held his giant-sized hand up and Morgan slapped it back with a big old "high five".

"Well, what are we waiting for, then, baby? Let's go get that million-dollar recipe!" Big Ed let out a hearty laugh as they headed out the door.

Detective Reuben had joined Captain Brown and Harry Phillips at the North Shore Hotel to review the surveillance video, and they were about to make an astonishing discovery of their own.

"Look! There's a woman leaving the building, and it looks like she's walking towards the beach!" Captain Brown pointed out. With all eyes glued on the surveillance camera monitor, they watched as a darkly dressed woman hurried out of Valli's office building and headed down to the public beach access just a few hundred feet away. They continued watching, as she ducked underneath the pier, and stooped down. Eyes bulging, they all three gasped at the same time.

"Oh my God! Look – she's burying something in the sand! The gun! She's burying that gun! That's GOT to be Jack's killer!" Captain Brown exclaimed excitedly. The woman then hurried off, until she was totally out of view of the camera.

"Harry, can you rewind one more time and try to zoom in a little closer on that girl leaving the building?" As the video zoomed in, he noticed a broad smile spread over Detective Reuben's face.

"What, Joe, what is it? Do you recognize that girl?"

"Yeah, I recognize her, but I never would have suspected HER!"

"What? You know who that girl is, Joe?"

"Well, not exactly, but I know where we can find her – that is unless she's skipped town!"

"Alright then – let's go get her! Harry, think you can send a copy of this video over to my office ASAP?"

"You got it, Frank! Anything to help catch a crook!"

"Thanks, Harry – I owe you one! C'mon, Joe – let's go arrest a murder suspect!!"

Chapter 18

"I don't feel right about this, Seth." Valli felt uneasy as she and Seth rummaged through Jack's desk drawers in his office at Heart Winery.

"For God's sake, why not, Val? We're just looking for something that is rightfully YOURS, remember?! That secret recipe is the property of Heart Winery, not to mention our future! Or have you forgotten why we've been sneaking around all these months? Don't you see – once we get that recipe, we don't have to sneak around anymore, and we can be free to show our true feelings in public without anyone being suspicious - AND, we can start planning our future together! Isn't that what you want now?"

"I don't know – it just doesn't seem right. Maybe we should just wait until the investigation is over. I'd hate to think what Detective Reuben would think if he caught us snooping around in here. It just makes us look even guiltier!"

"Guilty of WHAT? Murder? You still think I had something to do with Jack's murder, don't you? I swear, Valli - what have I got to do to make you believe me when I say I didn't kill Jack?!"

"No! I didn't mean that, Seth. I just don't think it's a good idea for us to be here right NOW – that's all. Detective Reuben said I wasn't to tamper with anything until the investigation was finished. Besides, they've already got Jack's computer and they'll probably come back for the files."

"That's even more reason we need to be here, Val – in case they DO come back for the files. If that recipe is in this office, we need to find it before they do! Our future depends on it, not to mention the future of Heart Winery. What if someone else finds it? Don't you realize how dangerous that could be? They could sell it to another company, or worse yet, destroy it! If that recipe gets in the wrong hands, it could be the end of Heart Winery. How could you let that happen to your father's company? Doesn't his memory mean more to you than that?"

Valli realized what Seth was saying was true. They HAD to get that recipe back in safe hands, even if it meant being deceptive to do it. Surely God would want her to do whatever she had to do to save her father's company! She just hoped they weren't too late.

"But what if the recipe isn't even here, Seth? What if Jack has it locked in a safety deposit box somewhere, or hidden somewhere at his apartment? We may NEVER find it!" Hearing a noise, Seth quickly covered Valli's mouth with his hand.

"Shh! I hear something – sounds like someone's coming! Quick – let's get in the closet!" He quickly shoved Valli in the coat closet in Jack's office. The office door hinges squeaked just a bit as the handle slowly turned, and the door to Jack's office opened. Seth and Valli scrunched up close together in the tiny closet and held their breath. They heard a husky voice speak.

"Make sure you lock that door behind you, sweetheart!" the man instructed.

"I did. Now start searching for that damn recipe!" a woman replied.

"Okay, you look in the desk and I'll go through these files."

While the intruders rummaged through desk drawers and file cabinets, Seth and Valli remained quiet as a mouse in the closet, afraid to move or make a sound. Valli took the opportunity to close her eyes and ask God for help, but all she could think about was how dishonest and deceptive she felt cowering in a coat closet in a dead man's office! Surely God didn't approve, and the guilt washed over her like a tidal wave. It was at that moment that she promised God if he would get her and Seth out of this mess alive, she would NEVER engage in any other deceptive plans ever again!

The intruders kept talking in a whispered voice, and Seth and Valli strained to keep up with the conversation from the cramped closet.

"Are you SURE it's even here?" The man sounded thoroughly disgusted with his obvious empty-handed search.

"Yeah, it's gotta be here. He told me so. Said it was safely hidden in his office" the woman replied.

"Yeah, well he could have been lying. He lied to you about an affair with that Heart woman, didn't he?" Suddenly, the woman noticed the closet that Seth and Valli were hiding in.

"Maybe it's in there!" she said, pointing to the closet.

It was then that Valli recognized Morgan's voice, but all she could do was tug at Seth's coat and mouth, "THAT'S MORGAN OLIVER!" Seth nodded in guarded surprise, then noticed the door handle to the closet start to turn. He wasn't sure what was going to happen next, but he knew he had to do something drastic!

As the closet door was about to open, Seth busted out, knocking the man to the floor. A fight broke out between the two men, but Seth was quick enough to grab a bottle of wine from the nearby bar and whack him over the head with it. The man fell to the floor – unconscious and with a badly cut and bleeding head. Valli slowly exited the closet she had been cowering in while the fight was going on.

"YOU??! What the... what are YOU doing here?" Morgan Oliver screamed when she realized Valli was standing in front of her.

"NO, Morgan the question is, what are YOU doing here? And how did YOU know about the secret recipe for the Blue Merlot? I heard every word you just said from the closet. And who's the big guy Seth just knocked out?"

Morgan was huddled over Big Ed, who was just coming to. She reared up and screamed at Valli. "I should have known you'd come looking for that recipe, too, you slut!"

Panicking, Morgan tried to make a run for the door, but Seth pulled a gun from his waistband and pointed it at her. Morgan froze in her tracks.

"Oh no, you're not going anywhere, sweetheart. Not until we get some answers! Val – call Detective Reuben and tell him to get down here right away! We might just have nabbed a couple of murder suspects for him!" Seth held the gun on Morgan and Big Ed while Valli quickly called Detective Reuben.

While Seth and Valli detained Morgan and Big Ed at Jack's office, Captain Brown and Detective Reuben pulled up to the I-95 Grill, sure they were about to crack the case.

"So, THIS is where she works?" Captain Brown asked detective Reuben as they parked the car.

"Yea, I caught a glimpse of her the first time I came in here looking for Morgan Oliver. I just hope she's still here!" As they got ready to get out of the car, Detective Reuben suddenly stopped.

"Wait, Frank – look – on the side of the building. That's her taking a smoke break! She IS still here! We got her!"

"Okay, take it easy, Joe. Let's not scare her off. We'll wait till she goes back in, then I'll go on in and see if I can find out who she is. You go around and slip in the back, in case she tries to make a run for it!"

A few minutes later, the girl finished her cigarette, and went back inside. Captain Brown and Detective Reuben quickly made their move. Once inside the diner, Captain Brown stayed out of view until he could identify the young girl they had seen outside. He nonchalantly asked another waitress who she was.

"Her? Oh, that's Jessie. Jessica Rose." The waitress then walked away, unconcerned over Captain Brown's interest in her co-worker. Captain Brown nodded in appreciation, then made his way over to Jessica Rose.

"Jessica Rose – you're under arrest for the murder of Jack Conova!" he said, quickly twisting her hand behind her back, and slapping the handcuffs on her wrists. Watching from the back room he had slipped into earlier, Detective Reuben immediately rushed in and assisted in the arrest.

"What?! What are you talking about? I ain't killed no one! Let me go!" Jessica screamed, struggling to get free, as they led her out to the squad car.

"Save it sister! We got you dead to rights, thanks to a little piece of surveillance video! The only thing we don't know is WHY you killed him. Maybe you can explain that part to us down at the station!" Detective Reuben replied, shoving her in the back of the patrol car. On the way to the station Detective Reuben received the call from Valli.

"Reuben, here. Oh, hello Ms. Heart, what's up?" His eyes widened in surprise at the news he was receiving. "Oh really? Don't leave – we're on the way! I'll call for backup!"

"What's that all about, Joe? Back up for WHAT?"

"We gotta make a little detour over to Heart Winery, Captain. Seems like "there's a big hide and seek game going on for some kind of secret wine recipe, and you'll never believe who's playing!"

Jessica Rose squirmed nervously in the back seat of the patrol car, as she watched her world slowly crumble right before her eyes. But she wasn't about the take the fall by herself. If SHE went down, they ALL did! No way would she go down alone!

Chapter 19

"YOU! YOU killed Jack, didn't you?!" Valli screamed at Morgan. "It all makes sense now. You've wanted revenge on Jack ever since you caught us together in my office that night, haven't you? Jack must have been in contact with you and told you he was meeting me in my office the night he was killed. So, you got there first, broke in and waited for him, then shot him when he came in. And he must have also told you about the secret recipe for the Blue Merlot wine, so you and that big goon over there decided to come over here and try to find it and sell it to another wine company. That's how you had it all figured out, isn't it Morgan? That's why you killed Jack, isn't it – for your own selfish revenge!"

"Oh, shut up, Valli! You don't know what you're talking about! I didn't kill Jack, and that stupid detective knows it because I've got an alibi. I was at work that night, and Big Ed over there vouched for me!" she explained, pointing to Big Ed, still lying crumpled and dazed on the floor.

"Then you must have had someone else to do your dirty work for you! Who was it, Morgan? Who was your trigger-man?" Morgan just stood there grinning at Valli. She wasn't about to give her the satisfaction of confessing to a crime she had worked so hard to pin on someone else.

Finally, Captain Brown and Detective Reuben arrived on the scene, with Jessica Rose in hand cuffs tagging along.

"What's going on here? Would someone care to explain what all you people are doing in Jack Conova's office, against Detective Reuben orders?" Captain Brown sternly asked.

"I'll tell you what's going on, Captain." Valli pointed sharply at Morgan. "That woman is Morgan Oliver, an EX-Heart Winery employee – AND a murderer! She and her boyfriend over there, "Big Ed," were trying to find the secret recipe for the Blue Merlot wine Jack developed so they could sell it and get rich! I want them BOTH arrested right this instant for trespassing – AND murder!"

"And just what are YOU and Mr. Spencer doing here?" Detective Reuben asked. Valli had the "deer in the headlights" look, but Seth quickly came to her defense.

"Valli is the CEO of Heart Winery, and it is her responsibility to see that her company is still running properly, despite Jack's death. She has every right to be here! Besides, didn't you hear what Valli said? Morgan Oliver is the one who killed Jack! Why else would she be here trying to get that recipe?"

"No, Mr. Spencer, she didn't kill Jack. But someone else in this room did." Detective Reuben held up Jessica Rose's handcuffed wrists.

"This is Jessica Rose – a friend and employee of Morgan and Big Ed's at the I-95 Grill. I recognized her on the surveillance video taken from the North Shore Hotel across the street. She was seen entering Ms. Heart's office building the night of the murder, before Jack Conova arrived, and then coming out a little while later. She was also seen running down to the beach and hiding a gun in the sand. We just picked her up at the I-95 Grille, right before Ms. Heart called and told us what was going on over here."

"I don't understand, Detective. Why would she want to kill Jack?" Valli was so sure Morgan was the murderer!

"That's what we don't know yet. We were on the way to take Ms. Rose to the station when you called. But now it seems like we're going to have to take Ms. Oliver and Big Ed in, to explain what they're doing here, as well!"

"I'll tell you what they're doing here – they're looking for that damn secret wine recipe! That was the plan, and I'm not going to take the fall for this whole thing myself!" Jessica Rose blurted out.

"Shut up, Jessie! You don't know what you're talking about! Big Ed and I were just looking for the diamond ring Jack gave me when we got married. I gave it back to him after I caught him screwing around with Valli, and now I want it back. We were going to sell it to pay off some bills, that's all!"

"LIAR!" Jessica Rose screamed at Morgan. "You're a lying bitch! I ain't taking the fall for this Morgan – no way in HELL are you getting off, leaving me to go to prison by myself! You're the one who cooked this whole deal up, and you know it! You just used me to kill Jack, so you wouldn't have to get your pretty little hands dirty, then you and Big Ed were going to make millions by selling that damn secret wine recipe, leaving me out of it all! You're a dirty double crosser and I hate you for getting me mixed up in all this!"

"Are you confessing to the murder of Jack Conova, Ms. Rose?" Detective Reuben asked. Jessica Rose stared defiantly at Morgan Oliver and slowly nodded her head, confessing to Jack's murder.

"Yeah, I killed him. But she bribed me to do it!" she confessed, pointing to Morgan. "She offered me ten thousand dollars if I would break into Valli's office and kill Jack, using the gun Big Ed bought from Seth Spencer. She told me to take the gun down to the beach and hide it in the sand, so someone would find it and turn it in. Then it would be traced back to Valli's boyfriend here, and they would both be implicated in Jack's murder! She wanted revenge on ALL of them, and this was her and Big Ed's plan. They just used me to do their dirty work – and for a lousy ten grand at that! But I ain't going to prison by myself so you might as well go ahead and arrest them too!"

Seth immediately recognized Big Ed as the guy he had sold the handgun to a year earlier. "So THAT'S why he wanted to buy MY gun! Morgan must have found out somehow that Valli and I were seeing each other. And Jack must have mentioned to her that I collected guns, so she sent Big Ed to buy one of my 9mm's, knowing all along they were going to kill Jack, and use my own gun to frame me his murder!"

"That's why you should ALWAYS run a background check on someone you're planning to sell a firearm too, Spencer!" Captain Brown chided. "And follow up to make sure they get it registered in THEIR name!"

"Yea, I'll remember that, Captain - thanks." Seth dropped his head in embarrassment, but relieved the truth was finally out.

Captain Brown nodded to the other officers who had been called for backup, and Morgan Oliver and Big Ed were taken into custody, along with Jessica Rose.

"Well, Mr. Spencer, it looks like you're off the hook. Our apologies for any inconvenience this whole ordeal has caused you and Ms. Heart."

"That's okay, Captain. We're just glad the REAL killer has been caught – and her accomplices!"

"That's right," Valli chimed in. "And I can't thank you enough for all your hard work in getting to the bottom of this. You not only helped saved OUR lives, but also the livelihood of Heart Winery! I am so grateful to you both!"

"All in a day's work, Ms. Heart. But we will still need both of you to come to the station and give your full testimonies, to bring full charges against these three."

"That is NOT a problem, Captain! Oh, and by the way, would it be possible to get Jack's computer and files sent back to his office, so we can get back to business around here?"

"I don't see why not, Ms. Heart. It doesn't look like we're going to need them now that we've got a full confession from Ms. Rose. You can pick them up when you come by the station."

Valli smiled at Seth and let out a deep sigh of relief. The nightmare was finally over – along with a few others that had haunted her all her life. Now that Jack's murder was solved, she and Seth could move forward with their lives and run Heart Winery together!

After Captain Brown and Detective Reuben left with Morgan, Big Ed and Jessica, Valli and Seth fell into each other's arms, emotionally exhausted and spent, but relieved and excited about their future ahead.

EPILOGUE

"It's finally over, my love!" Seth whispered the precious words Valli had longed to hear for so long, as he held her tightly in his arms back at his yacht.

"See, I told you they would figure out everything in the end. I'm just so sorry it had to have such a devastating ending for old Jack. Although I never liked him, I never wanted him dead – or dreamed anyone ever would kill him!"

"I know, I still can't believe he's dead. But Jack was only after one thing – and that was my father's company! I just thank God that you were here, Seth. I don't know if I could have handled Jack if you hadn't been here for me all along."

"Well, I'm not going anywhere, sweetheart, so you may as well get used to having me around! But we've still got to find that recipe if we want to keep Heart Winery alive and prosperous!"

"You know what Seth? God knows where that recipe is, and I'm just going to pray that He reveals to us where it is. And I know that if it's His will for us to find it, he'll show us where to look. But for now, I'm tired of thinking about it. Can't we just relax and forget about it for now?"

"Of course, darling. You must be exhausted from all this. And you're right. God has taken us this far, and He's not about to let us down now. That recipe will show up soon, I'm sure of it!" With that quiet assurance, Valli fell fast asleep in Seth's arms, and for once, rested peacefully throughout the night without the need for even one sanity pill!

Bright and early the next day, Valli and Seth went down to the police station to give their testimonies. While there, they retrieved Jack's computer and files, and carried them back to his office. For hours, they scoured and combed computer files and documents looking for the recipe for the Blue Merlot, but it just didn't seem anywhere to be found. Jack knew how valuable that recipe was and had hidden it well. Valli's hopes of ever finding it were quickly dashed. While Seth was still looking, she closed her eyes and prayed.

"Dear God, you know how important that recipe is to the success and longevity of Heart Winery. Even though we went to extreme and even unethical means to keep Jack from taking over this company, I'm asking you to forgive us for our sins, and show us where to find that recipe so it won't fall into the wrong hands. Please, for my father's sake, help us find it! Amen."

"I just don't know what he could have done with it, Val. He must have shoved it in a wine bottle and threw it in the ocean!" Suddenly, a lightning bolt from heaven hit Valli! Never had God answered one of her prayers so quickly!

"C'mon, honey – I think I know where the recipe is!" she exclaimed excitedly, dragging Seth by one arm out of Jack's office and down the hall.

"Where? Where are we going, Val?"

"Down to the wine cellar! I think I know where Jack may have hidden the secret recipe!"

The wine cellar at Heart Winery held some of the oldest and most prized vintage bottles of wine since Heart Winery's beginning, like the first bottle of wine ever bottled by her father when he took over the business from her Grandfather Heart. It was a well secured, protected and climate-controlled room, and the perfect place to keep a secret recipe!

"So, why do you think the recipe is in here?"

"Oh, I just do," Valli replied confidently. "Look, over here!" She walked over to a locked display case of vintage wines arranged in order by year. At the very end of the display stood a bottle of Blue Merlot.

"See – there it is – the Blue Merlot!"

"Yea, so it's a bottle of Blue Merlot. So, what? I don't get it, Valli," Seth answered in a bewildered tone.

Valli fished in her pocket for her keys, unlocked the display case and lifted the lid. She removed the Blue Merlot bottle and closed the case. She gently shook the bottle and held it up to the light.

"Yep – just as I thought! Quick, hand me that corkscrew over there on the bar!"

Seth handed her a corkscrew and she gently pried the cork from the bottle of Blue Merlot and turned the bottle upside down. A long glass cylinder containing a long scroll of paper fell into her hands. She carefully unrolled the scroll to reveal the secret recipe to the Blue Merlot wine! Her eyes sparkled and danced with excitement as she held the paper up to Seth.

"See! I told you God would show us where it was! And it's been here all the time!" Seth was amazed at her timely intuition.

"But how did you know to look here?"

"Well, I remember Jack saying one time that all these wines were the "heart and soul" of Heart Winery, and that one day the Blue Merlot would earn its rightful place in this display case along with all the others. Then when he came up with that slogan about "putting his heart and soul" into Blue Merlot, I guess he figured it had earned its spot here! And he knew this case was locked and protected, so I guess he figured it was the perfect place to hide the recipe. I mean who would have guessed there was anything in this bottle but wine?"

"Well, not me, for one! Ms. Heart, you are a GENIUS, if you don't mind me saying so!"

"Why, thank you, Mr. Spencer for that kind compliment! And now that we've got the recipe, there's just one more piece of unfinished business I need to attend to." Staring deeply and lovingly into Seth's eyes, she spoke the tender words he longed to hear.

"Darling, if it hadn't been for you, I know Jack would have ruined this company. I will be forever grateful to you for that, and I know my father would be too. I know it was our plan all along, but I'm officially making you the Vice President and Co-Owner of Heart Winery right now! Please say you'll accept the position and help me run Heart Winery from here on out!"

Seth tenderly brushed a stray hair from her face, then sweetly kissed her forehead.

"Valli Heart, I would be honored to work alongside you, my darling! I promise you I will make it my lifelong commitment to do everything possible to make sure Heart Winery is run with all the professionalism, integrity and intelligence your father would have wanted. I know I can never fill his shoes, but I would be proud and honored to follow in his footsteps! Furthermore, we will take Blue Merlot to the Crescent Beach Wine Festival this year and bring back FIRST place!"

He leaned down and kissed Valli slowly and deliberately, and with all the passion of a man who was deeply in love. Valli melted in his kiss, finally able to release all the pent-up anguish and anxiety she had carried with her for over twenty-five years. She finally realized that when Jack died, so did all the devils and demons that had haunted her for so long.

For now, she didn't have to live in shame or embarrassment over her past sins; afraid of them rearing their ugly heads to destroy her future. She finally felt safe and loved in Seth's arms, and ready to release her heart from the "sealed bottle" that had held it captive for so long.

THE END

"Peace I leave with you, my peace I give unto you: not as the world giveth, give I unto you. Let not your heart be troubled, neither let it be afraid."

– John 14:27 KJV

About the Author

Lisa A. Tippette is a self-published Bohemian Christian romance author from North Carolina, and *Heart in a Bottle* is her third published novel. Lisa developed a natural love for writing at an early age by keeping a diary, like most young girls her age. For hours on end, she would hide away in her bedroom closet with her diary and write down her deepest thoughts and secrets. She continued to write throughout her early school years, winning several writing awards, and honed her writing skills by taking creative writing courses. As an adult, she retained her love for writing, and eventually went on to self-publish her first novelette – ***Broken Dreams and Answered Prayers***, later followed by her second book, ***Letting Go: Emily's Homecoming***. (Both available on Amazon.com)

Lisa has a unique and gifted ability to create dynamic dialogue between characters that draws the reader into the story and makes them feel as if they are a part of it – not just reading it. Her creative descriptive abilities paint a perfect picture for each story, and brings her books to life, page after page. Although her writing passion is for fiction Christian romance novels, she has also written beautiful poetry, inspirational works and personal blogs on numerous internet writing venues.

Currently, Lisa owns her own successful website design company, and is a social media consultant. She also has a love for photography, and is an amateur nature photographer, with a special passion for photographing beach landscape and ocean scenes. Many of her prints can be viewed and purchased on Fine Art America.com, as well as Flickr.com and other internet photo sites.

Lisa resides in Enfield, North Carolina, with her husband Robbie, and their rescue fur-child, a high-spirited Box-ador named Bubba.

To contact Lisa, please email her at

mybohemiantypewriter@gmail.com

Other Books You May Enjoy by Lisa A. Tippette:

Broken Dreams and Answered Prayers © 2012

Letting Go: Emily's Homecoming © 2013

Keep up with Lisa, her writings and purchase her books by visiting her blog/website:

www.bohemiantypewriter.com

HELP SUPPORT INDIE AUTHORS!

If you enjoyed this book, please help support the Indie author who wrote it by reviewing it on your social media pages, Amazon (if purchased online), or through my website, **www.bohemiantypewriter.com.**

Thank you for buying, reading, and reviewing Indie publications!

83132495R00072

Made in the USA
Lexington, KY
10 March 2018